RAW MATERIAL

M.A.C. FARRANT

RAW MATERIAL

ARSENAL PULP PRESS
Vancouver, Canada

RAW MATERIAL

ARSENAL PULP PRESS
100-1062 Homer Street
Vancouver, B.C.
Canada V6B 2W9

The publisher gratefully acknowledges the assistance of the Canada Council and the Cultural Services Branch, B.C. Ministry of Tourism and Minister Responsible for Culture.

This is a work of fiction. Any resemblance to situations or persons living or dead is amazingly coincidental.

Author photo by Terry Farrant
Typeset by the Vancouver Desktop Publishing Centre
Printed and bound in Canada by Hignell Printing

CANADIAN CATALOGUING IN PUBLICATION DATA:
Farrant, M. A. C. (Marion Alice Coburn), 1947-
Raw material

ISBN 0-88978-262-8

I. Title.
PS8561.A76S9 1993 C813'.54 C93-091292-6
PR9199.3.F37S9 1993

CONTENTS

ACKNOWLEDGEMENTS

These fictions first appeared in the following magazines: "Swing" and "The Teapot Shudders" in *paragraph;* "Song For Leonard Cohen" and "Philosopher's Mix" in *Exile;* "Song for Leonard Cohen" appeared in *Random Thought;* "The Early Plastic Shrine" and "The Two Gentle Ladies From K- Mart" in *Rampike;* "The Children Do Not Yet Know" in *On Spec: The Canadian Magazine of Speculative Fiction;* "FISH" in *On Spec* and the Australian anthology *Going Down Swinging* (Hit and Miss Press, 1992); "Etiquette" in *What!;* "Free Enterprise" in *Front Magazine* (Western Front); "Studies Show/Experts Say" in *Mental Radio;* "The Mouse Incident," "Beige" and "Street" in *Existere;* "Happy Birthday" in *Next Exit;* "The Bright Gymnasium of Fun" in *Adbusters Quarterly* (entitled "Laughter").

"Raw Material," "childless" and "Poor Norman" appeared as chapbooks produced by David UU for The Berkeley Horse (Silver Birch Press) (1989, 1990 and 1991). "Bed" is forthcoming from TBH in 1994 as part of a series entitled "Three." "Saucers" appeared in the chapbook *M A C,* produced by damian lopes for fingerprinting inkoperated (1992).

"The Early Plastic Shrine," "bed," "Happy Birthday" and "childless" appeared in the anthology *Snapshots: The New Canadian Fiction* (Black Moss Press, 1992).

Special thanks to the following people for their continued support: Pauline Holdstock, David UU, Vicky Husband, Joan Henriksen, Norman Wright, Terry Farrant; to Jane Powell and Carol Van Andrichem for sending work my way during lean times; and to Bob and Doreen Jones for (yikes!) the executive desk and chair.

For my daughter, Anna
and my son, Bill

The essential things in life fall from heaven and remain floating just above any possible basis of explanation. Let us say that out of an obscure impulse of *joie de vivre* and melancholy, experienced together as a climax of life, is born a mood that we call the festive mood and in which we enjoy total freedom.

—C. Verhoeven,
The Philosophy of Wonder

THE TEAPOT SHUDDERS

for David UU

O*h no, not another malevolent vine scratching at the window. This one has flowers, the sickly white, enticing flowers of the* Armandi Clematis *groping its way along the outside ledge, pressing its putrid stamens onto the window pane. Look outside to the window, I say. (Can't disguise the alarm in my voice.) You, you merely yawn, preferring to recall your distant past. The time your uncle took your sister and you to Chinatown on Christmas day. Your sister was six, you were only ten. Took you to the crummiest place on earth, a restaurant with sleeping drunks, where light bulbs swayed from fraying cords above your tiny heads, where the smell of fish was everywhere and now you hate the taste as well. I've heard it all a hundred times. Your uncle drinking rye from a Chinese cup then nodding off and, drooling, hits the floor. The fear, the thrill. The search through his pockets for the rescuing dime. The phone call home. A horror story safely told. (Can't disguise the horror in my voice.) Just look outside to the window, I say, the* Armandi *is hugely growing, is about to cover the window, possibly the house. Even while we speak it's sucking the light from our eyes, making it dark and dangerous at the breakfast table. The teapot shudders, the knives and spoons are melting* *with fear. What should have been an alive morning sunny with hope could now disappear altogether. Hope is hugely over-rated, you say. Its sickly fingers, the way it gropes, the way its victims pant for death. I've heard it all a hundred times. The fear, the thrill. And there are many ways to kill a plant, all of them wonderful.*

POOR NORMAN

Everywhere you turn there are devices to capture your imagination. I love it. Norman can't stand it but I love it. Love it. Love it. It drives Norman mad so he keeps to the house now, locked in our bedroom closet.

I have a birthday present for Norman. A pair of orange ear protectors, the kind our neighbours use when they mow their lawns. We, of course, don't have a lawn, we have a jungle. This is because Norman won't come out of the closet and do the mowing. He says a freshly cut lawn is the sign of a captured imagination. Our grass is a nasty tangle of thistle and weed scratching at our living room window.

I can still remember Norman's words to me the night he went into the closet for good:

> . . . The captured imagination elects other
> captured imaginations to keep what is in
> all of their minds, captured.

Poor Norman. Now he'll be able to wear his new ear protectors while he's in the bedroom closet. That way he won't hear my TV. He particularly hates the commercials. I love them. I know all the tunes. Go on, just ask me one. I could sing them all day long. Sometimes I do. They soothe me, those little mind grabbers.

> . . . curl it, curl it, make it hot, girl . . .

Norman has sawed an opening, knee-high, in the closet door. That's how I pass him his food. It's a big closet, what the sales agent called a walk-in closet, attached to the ensuite. A retirement dream. Norman's been in there for four years.

Before that he was in business. Men's clothing. When you think of it, a kind of closet, too. All those racks of suits and sports coats. All those years of fumbling through the wools and acrylic blends: Charcoal Grey, Midnight Blue, the Summer Tans, the Plaids. I suppose Norman feels at home in the closet. The way I feel at home before the TV set with my knitting.

. . . I've got a friend, not the usual kind . . .

That time I forgot to take my pill, I woke in the night to find Norman standing beside my bed, staring out the bedroom window. A frightening sight. A beard. So much hair. His formally neat fringe grown down past his neck, lying on his shoulders like limp string. And fat, he was. Like a large, pale toad.

Perhaps he was staring out at our retirement camper parked beside the house, it's wheels lost in the swaying grass. It's never been used.

I wonder if Norman comes out of the closet every night. That would explain things. Someone has been melting the gold decoration off my china tea cups and replacing it with common yellow paint. Someone has been spraying our oak trees in the front yard with oil and they're dying. Often I awake in the morning to find my knitting all unravelled and deposited in a neat pile at the foot of the bed as if some woolly night time monster had relieved himself of it there. Norman's Christmas vest. The grey one I knit him every year. The special one with the difficult cable stitch.

Sometimes there's a note from Norman on his supper tray. Today's note said:

. . . The captured imagination cannot remember
how it got captured but believes it has
something to do with God.

So I crouched by the closet and sang at him through the opening.

. . . From off the mountain and into your cup . . .
Juan Valdez gathers the beans for Maxwell House . . .

I love Juan Valdez. Love him. Love him. We meet on the sunny, green hillsides of South America. I take the train, the one with the open windows and the crowds of grinning natives. To find him, swarthy and alone, crouched over his rows of coffee plants, gathering beans for Maxwell House. He always smiles when he sees me, holding one perfect bean up to the sunlight for me to admire. The blessing in his kind, brown face . . .

I'm going to gift wrap Norman's orange ear protectors. I hope he wears them. Then he won't complain about my singing for Juan Valdez. Won't hear the hammering when I seal up the closet for good.

FISH

for Vicky Husband

By day, carrying on with my fish body assembly work. By night, waking to find strangers in my bed. Last night, Mrs. Hanson and her three kids. A trail of a person.

Rip doesn't seem to mind the strangers. He just rolls over, grumbles about needing more covers, leaving me to contend.

By day, all is well. The important fish body assembly work continuing. But three nights ago, an elderly couple vacationing from Alberta. He bald and snoring, she in hair net pondering. Maps and guidebooks spread out all over the quilt.

It's the nighttime crowds I can't stand. Whole families

arguing. Some under the covers with Rip and me, others sitting on the bedside nattering.

It gets worse when I sweat because of too many people. Then I have to throw off the covers and everyone starts in on me then, complaining. Many of the strangers don't like our bedroom, for instance: no proper dresser, a doorless closet, the bed merely a double. I wish I wouldn't apologize so much. *Feel so responsible.*

"Perhaps if I cleaned up the room you'd feel better," I say. "Perhaps if I slept on the floor next to the dog."

More room for Mrs. Hanson and the three kids. Mrs. Hanson slithering naked next to Rip. Mrs. Hanson breathing lullabies into Rip's dozing face.

By day I'm a person of importance. Thank heavens. With my fish body assembly work. Nearly fifty thousand so far and the numbers keep climbing. The parts from Hong Kong, duty free. That was my doing. I found the rule about location making it is permissible for a manufacturer to assemble a product on home turf thus avoiding import tax. The rule book was old but not forgotten. I take pride in that. Ferreter of antique rules.

The woman at Customs agreed, but not wholeheartedly.

"Right here on page fifteen of ENTRY REQUIREMENTS FOR PARTS FROM FOREIGN PARTS," I showed her.

She wasn't happy. They don't like to give anything away. They come to believe it's *their* rule you're tampering with.

"It's a nice rule," I told her, "one you should be proud of."

But she took it personally. That the government would be missing out on its due tax. That's dedication for you.

We all get on. Somehow. Me, I'm doing my part for the environment. Tax free. And I won't have to charge sales tax on the assembled fish bodies either because I won't be selling them. Because, in a sense, I'll be giving them away.

Rip was disappointed I didn't use my inheritance money for something more worthwhile. That's his opinion. A jazz trio, for example. I know he's always wanted one of those. Piano, bass, drums. Playing Bill Evans on demand. Actually he'd like to have Bill Evans as well. I've often hoped he'd visit us in bed but the dead can be very stubborn. So far, no show.

A Bill Evans tape wouldn't do. I suggested it.

"Too small," Rip said.

He wants to be wrapped in the live thing, ear to the electric bass speaker or sit beside the piano player and stroke his fingers while he's playing. Or crouch beneath the piano player's legs and work the peddle. Involvement. That's what Rip wants.

But I only had enough inheritance money for one of us to be involved. And after all. It's important to me that I calm things down. Quit my job at the gas station just so I could take the time.

The fish bodies are all the same size. Ten inches. Just

under the legal size limit. Plastic. Overall grey in colour, made up of three sections: head, shaft, tail. Flecks of pink and blue in the plastic. Could be mistaken for a trout, a cod or a young salmon. That's not the important part, the type. It's just so *they can be seen to be there.*

I've always wanted to raise spirits.

Getting tired, though, with all these strangers turning up in our bed. I tell Rip about it but he just gets annoyed.

"Don't be so rigid," he says, "have a little flexibility. After all, they're not bothering you, are they? Not in any significant way? Beating you about the head or sitting on your back? Complaints about the bedroom furniture don't count. They're not actually hurting you, are they?"

Apart from Mrs. Hanson's gymnastics over Rip's body last night, I'd have to say, no, they're not.

"Well then," he says, "be like a rock in a stream, a tree in a storm. Let your turmoil flow around and away from you."

That's my Rip. He'd be a Zen Buddhist if he had the time. As it is, he's run off his feet. No wonder he sleeps through the night time visitors. By day, he's selling Bic Pens, Eddy Matches. He's got the whole territory from here to Burgoyne Bay and having the whole of anything is exhausting. So there's always someone in *his* bed. *In a manner of speaking.*

He's right, though. I make too big a deal about everything. Always have. Still.

Seven members of the Golden Eagles Day Camp the

night before last. Out on an adventure sleepover with their Counsellor.

Children are far too active, especially in sleep. Why I've never gone in for them. One of the campers tried to cuddle next to me, one even tried to climb into my arms. Rip just shoved them aside as if they were sleeping cats, heavy lumps. But me, I can't. I've always got to be taking charge. Half the night gone running back and forth to the fridge—juice for the campers. And then the nineteen-year-old counsellor having trouble with her boyfriend and wanting to talk. By morning I was a wreck from trying to keep everyone happy.

I can't leave well enough alone. Or in this case, bad enough alone. Doing my bit for the environmental movement. I can't stand it when people get upset. The depleting fish stocks. All the hue and cry.

My bit. Keeping the complainers happy. I have parts for one hundred and fifty thousand fish bodies. The boxes are stacked in the living room, hallway, kitchen, down the stairs to the basement. Thought of using Mini-Storage but the inheritance money is running low. If I were a midget, it would seem like a cardboard city inside our house. Towers of boxes, alleyways dark and spooky, no telling what goes on in there.

One of the campers got lost the other night on the way to the bathroom. Found her wandering terrified amongst the tail sections.

I'm especially happy about those tail sections. After all those faxes to Mr. Ni in Hong Kong.

"They've got to look like they're swimming," I faxed. "They've got to look like they're *moving in schools through the water.*"

Mr. Ni is a marvel. Even without an engineer he managed to come up with a propeller thingy that's connected to an elastic band. And he guarantees it. Either my assembled fish bodies self-propel or he'll take them back. That's business. So far, on my bathtub trials, success. Except for an occasional turn of swimming on their backs. You just pull this elastic band, the tails whirl and away they go.

I was trying to tell Mrs. Hanson about my plans last night in bed but she wasn't interested. Just wanted me to give the baby his bottle so she could get on with Rip's body rub.

The baby listened. "I will be delivering the first fifty thousand fish bodies by month's end," I told him. "I'm so excited. Rip has agreed to drive the hired truck. A dump truck. My plan is to back down the ramp at Anchor's Aweigh Marina about three in the morning. Only problem is, first I have to activate the tail sections. Otherwise, plunk, to the bottom of the deep blue sea."

Fifty thousand elastic bands snapping. I have to admit it's daunting. I'd have a nightmare about it, no doubt, if my nights weren't already so crowded. That's something. Too bad the strangers are always gone in the morning. I'm at the point where I could do with some help.

Right now what I picture before me is a string of busy, solitary days activating fish bodies. Their writhing grey forms mounting the cardboard box towers, scraping against the ceiling. Jiggling jelly. Maggot movement.

What keeps me going is *the thought.* All those upset people calmed down. Perhaps even happy. *Look, there's fish in the sea!* Again. After all. In spite of.

THE CHILDREN DO NOT YET KNOW

The children do not yet know what goes on beneath the sheets. We, of course, visit there regularly because that is where the airport is, and, as you get older, the flights you can take there become more and more appealing.

Right now, the children believe that something titillating goes on beneath the sheets, although they don't know this for sure. Grave gropings, perhaps, or the warm sponge of torsos, buttocks and breasts.

We do not plan, as yet, to tell the children about the airport because we feel that they should wait their turn. After all, they have a fair bit of youth ahead of them and won't be interested in flight until they are done tramping around in the awkward mud of concrete things: mortgages, income tax returns and the like.

Our friends feel the same way as we do. It's a favourite topic with us at our backyard barbecues: when to tell the children about the airport. We are all in favour of waiting until they are fully adult and then presenting the airport to them as a kind of consolation prize for responsible, middle-class living.

We first found the way to the airport by accident, under my husband's pillow, and a welcome discovery it was. I banged my head on it—my husband trying to squeeze new life out of an old situation—and, yes, I would have to say that since we have found the airport, a new intensity has entered into our marriage.

We spent weeks just trying to pry open the solid oak door (much grunting, much straining) and then several more clearing the descending wooden staircase of debris and repairing loose planks.

When we finally reached the airport we were enchanted. A white-washed tarmac stretching for miles toward a distant horizon, a flat mega-canvas dotted here and there with the shining forms of silver aircraft. Overhead, a cloudless sky. And not another person in sight. We immediately ran in different directions, my husband to a B-52 Bomber and I to a sweet, twin-engined Cessna with wings decorated to look like the wings of a butterfly, yellow and orange, much like the fabric design on our patio furniture.

The best flights, we have since found, are night flights, although we have been known to slip down for a quick one on a hot, sleepy afternoon.

Very often the children will be out building something in the back yard, a stadium, say, out of old boards and upturned flower pots or a vast city-complex out of empty margarine containers, cookie boxes and GI Joe tanks. I might be in the kitchen doing up the lunch dishes and my husband, standing at the kitchen window looking out at our children.

He might say to me very quietly, "Feel like a short flight, Barbara?" and I, smiling coyly and glancing towards the window, might say, "Well, Raymond, if you think there's enough time . . ."

We have many flights to choose from. There's The Run Away From Home Flight, The Adulterous Affair With Gummy Genitalia Flight, The Chorus Line And The Lonely Businessman Flight, The Family Flight, The Rescue Flight (a heaving sea of red jello) and The Vampire With The Enormous Penis Flight. These are some of our favourites.

Our friends like to visit our airport and we like to visit theirs. We have a great many friends and they are all, like us, unremarkable in the general silence of things. Many times when I drive through the city and see the crowds of unremarkable people going about their business, I wonder what it is that keeps us all like-minded. TV was my first thought but now I know it to be the airport. Having an airport beneath our bed sheets is the best kept secret of unremarkable people.

My husband continues to be quite definite about waiting to tell the children about the airport. Every time he returns from a flight, he tells me this. You see, he spends a great many hours away from his sales job sitting in the corner of our living room reading books on magic to impress the children but they remain unimpressed by the fantastic. Faeries, splendid castles, secret doors are a solid bore to them; they want the full dose of palpable reality. Fantastic to our children is the existence of the San Francisco Giants, or the black garbage truck that prowls our street on Mondays, or the World Atlas with its peacock display of nation flags in the index, or the thrill of commerce—having their own garage sales. It is only unremarkable, middle-aged adults like us who are lured by the fantastic: you spend half your life trying to dominate the physical world and the rest of it trying to forget what you know.

So we are very happy to have found our airport. And before long, when our children have become unremarkable adults themselves, they will be able to experience the airport, too. At that time, a final mystery for them will be solved. They will understand why, for all these years, their father and I have been so eager to go to bed in the evenings. Why we must have our Ovaltine at nine. Why our reading material must be arranged on the bedside table just so. Why the pillows must be plumped and the feather quilt made smooth to resemble a white-washed tarmac. These are all the preparations which my husband and I regularly take so that at midnight, if all is quiet in the household, we can join hands and descend the long, wooden staircase to our airport and the purring FA-117 Stealth Bomber that awaits us there.

BEIGE

Everything is beige. I'm glad of it. My walls, my floor. I've very happy about it. The siding on my house. This state of things has my strongest approval. Now I lay me down to sleep. Between beige sheets. Beside Mr. Beige, my husband, giving full reign to my beigeness. My beigeness will not be checked. It runneth over. God himself approves. Beige runneth from the end of my fingertips in long, dancing streamers fading everything I touch.

Beige; n. tan, biscuit, ecru (light brown); kinds of fabric made of undyed and unbleached wool; colour of this. Origin unknown.

I know. God has sent us beige. It is the neutral state of

things. It is calmness in the face of 'colour.' There is too much 'colour' in the world. Causing emotions. Causing Red and Yellow. Causing Blue. Blue makes my ears pound. Don't say 'colour' too loudly. Don't say 'colour' in capital letters. 'Colour' has a way . . . COLOUR . . . NO! . . . NO! . . . I told you not to say it . . . COLOUR . . . COLOUR . . . or else . . . NO! . . . Now you've done it. Here comes smarty-pants Pink . . . and violent Purple . . . and mean-spirited Yellow. Here come those garish Rainbows, Mr. & Mrs. with their ultra violet flock. Humming at me. Pulling at my retinas. Dizzying me with their lewdness. Lime Greenness. Raspberry Redness.

Hurry up. Give me my cardboard box, the one my beige dishwasher came in. Let me have my box so I can crawl in.

There. That's better. I'm in my box. Staring out the open end at my tranquil beige wall. I'm better now.

I've sucked the hue, tint, cast, shade, tinge and nuance out of the 'c'-word. All beige now. It's a wonder more people don't go in for it. A beige world would be a better world. For a start it would be bloodless. My world is bloodless. Now that I have my box.

Don't worry about me. I'm quite comfortable in here. Mr. Beige will bring me my supper. I just won't think about . . . you-know-what. I'll think about this:

Beige wall to wall
Maple walnut ice-cream
Chicken gravy

BEIGE

Camel hair coats
Mother-of-the-bride dresses
Old lace
Faded blondes
Oatmeal
Digestive cookies
Sawdust
Dust storms
Paper bags
Toothpicks
Dead grass

THE COMMA THREAT

I'm using up all my commas. I have a box of them sitting on my desk and I'm using them up. Well, I've given them away, as well. I gave some to my aunt to decorate her curtains; she flung handfuls of them against her drapes hoping for a Jackson Pollock effect. My son used one hundred and fifty of them for his science project on 'The Way Rain Falls,' using them like nails to tack down his subject. (I hated to deny him, though his use savaged my supply.) Then my mother-in-law asked to borrow at least twenty because she wanted to lengthen some sentences she was using in her Bridge game. There were some nifty bids she had in mind for her partner, she said, involving spades and top boards. She thought they'd have a real advantage if she added some commas, throwing off the competition who speak only in single words, such as "Pass" and "Hearts." And how could I say no to my mother-in-law who regularly lets me use her semi-colons?

But commas—those strong enough to withstand the rigors of fiction—are hard to come by. This is my problem: where to find a reliable supply. My neighbour picks up the odd bag-full for me from where she works at the school. She finds the commas fallen from textbooks and lying on the floor or blown in drifts beneath the blackboards. Old commas. They are from the time of ancient civilizations, from the Social Studies books, but they are prone to cracking. You put them in your sentence and before you know it, they have fallen off and a heap of them have collected at the bottom of the page. Commas from Social Studies books will just not stick so I've given up on them.

The same can be said of libraries. The whole world knows that libraries are comma-museums, the place where millions of commas have their final resting place. Just go to the section that houses 19th-century literature and you will be awash in commas. But, again, these are old, breakable commas and of little value. You could remove them by the wheel-barrow-full and no one would care. In fact, you'd be doing the library staff a favour; already they are knee deep in the commas that regularly fall from the pages of Dickens, Thackery and Henry James. It's appaling to realize what librarians must wade through in order to perform their book-tending duties.

The best commas come from letters of resignation, letters of termination, but these are private commas and difficult to get hold of. Still, they are likely to have the most effect in a piece because they are a substantial, finalizing sort of comma, very black in colour, and they never crack. They're the *lignum vitae* of commas, strong, and much prized if they can be found. They add a certain bleak seriousness to a piece, something I regularly covet. These commas are solid but insidious, like tics, those burrowing tics picked up on forest walks. The only way to get them out is to turn them slowly, counter-clockwise.

But don't tell a reader that. You start having a reader remove commas from your piece and before you know it, your words will be smashed up against each other. Panic overtakes first one sentence, then another, and then they all start rushing for the exit. The effect is domino: herds of sentences running amok through your book. Punctuation is slaughtered. It's really awful to see—all those commas strewn in the margins, leaking from the spines of books. It can have a negative effect on periods, too: it really shatters their sense of solidity. Capital letters automatically get scared and shrink. And exclamation marks! It's shocking to discover how really spineless they are. Exclamation marks will jump up and run at the slightest whiff of comma-threat; you'll find them huddled together on the back cover by the bar code. They just cannot hold their own in a sea of fluid words.

So the whole text is in jeopardy if a reader starts messing with the commas. Before you know it the sentences will have congealed into a large, black, amorphous mass and a void is created. And if you didn't realize it before now, *this* is how voids are created—by removing commas from a piece of fiction. Try removing the commas from this piece and see what happens. I won't be responsible, though, if you sink beneath the *and*s and *the*s, if you get trampled by the sudden, explosive rhythm that is unleashed, if you lose your way. Your cries for help won't be heard above the shrieks of quotation marks begging to be saved.

No, it's better if you leave the commas alone. They have a calming effect on a piece. Understand that commas are prized because they are a friend of time, slowing down the catapult, reigning in the breathless. Use them decoratively,,,,,,,,,as in this sentence,,,,,,,or use them sparingly. Too many commas in a piece can cause tripping, too few, an unnecessary strain on the heart. Balance must be achieved between word-intake, contemplation, and the always-hoped-for fireworks display in the reader's mind. Commas do this by slowing down the universe just long enough for the light to shine through; they are little warriors hammering away at chaos.

And now their existence is threatened. It all started with Gertrude Stein who was not impressed with commas and felt that if you're going to pause with a thought you might just as well end it. Written advertising picked up this theme, as did the minimalists with their sleek, exquisite sentences. But, in doing so, commas were lost and, over a scant fifty-year period, the supply of good quality commas has dwindled. Sure, there are still plenty of commas around. Look in any book that specializes in adjectives, in descriptions of coastal villages, barns, and the like. But these commas are a dime a dozen, flimsy, insubstantial commas. Digest commas, temporary commas. They don't stick. Not on the page. Not in the mind. Not anywhere.

Occasionally I've gotten a small number of commas from modernist texts. They're scant but thoughtfully placed. And because they're fairly new, they maintain their shine and can really dignify a piece. But it's hard work, retrieving modernist commas, like chipping paint from a window sill. You need a small chisel with a fine point, a pair of tweezers (or medical forceps) and a steady hand. It's time-consuming work, very often resulting in ripped pages. And some of those modernist commas will not budge, especially the cocky Hemingway commas which tend to fight to the death to stay on the page; you really need a washer-woman's strength to remove them. I have a set of twelve Hemingway trophy-commas which I'm saving for a special occasion. Each one is wrapped carefully in white tissue paper and set in two rows inside a black, velvet-lined case. Their procurement was the result of years of trial and error to discover the right attitude before the page: a bottle of Pernod, a canvas writing outfit, a rugged aloneness. "Comma to Momma," I might have said; it was amazing the way they surrendered.

But the supply problem persists. In fact, I've just used my last comma in this sentence after the word fact and you know what will happen now because already the periods are getting restless already the quotation marks are breathing heavy the whimpers from the text can almost be heard and it s too late to use those commas I so recklessly splashed about earlier in this piece the ones I wasted talking about comma decoration how foolish how insane to squander commas like that and now the whole text threatens to melt like jelly down a drain so do me a favour will you i ve just lost the question marks and capital letters do me a favour and send me any good quality commas you may have in your possession i don t care if they re used it doesn t matter if they re broken even half a comma would help but please before these words completely overtake me please send what ever you have my mind is going slack i beg you the words are in revolt send more commas these words won t behave they re forgetting where to place themselves and now they re runningforthehillslike

PICTURE

The Queen of England is in hubby's bed. She was visiting and asked if she could have a rest and I think she must have come last night. It's a crisis and I've gone from room to room but can't find anyone to explain things. Just some partying men in room number one. Just some newborn shoes in room number two. Just some wounded soldiers in room number three, four gentle boys with blood on their arms. Just hubby and Mellish in room number five. Smelly Mrs. Mellish who lives next door and hubby standing guard with his penis drawn, six feet long and stretching. But can't find anyone to explain things. Like where shall I put the Queen for tea? And what if she wants to inspect the men? And who's going to paint her portrait in oils? And why am I in this picture frame? This seven-by-eight-foot picture frame with nine white daisies in my hand. And why am I called still wife with flowers? And where is the one who'll explain things? I've ten more questions to ask yet. They're roaming from room to room now deciding where to hang me.

SWING

Ryan P. is a total nerd who runs with his feet sticking out like a duck. Plus he's always saying these gross things like how inside every blackberry there's a spider and if you swallow one you'll die. We hate him. We hate him to bits. I've checked every blackberry since he said this and I've never once found a single spider. I've even asked Elaine, my wife, about it and she said, Don't be stupid, so Ryan P. is a liar, too. On top of being a total idiot.

And now he's in front of me in the swing line.

And he doesn't even have a degree. All he's got is fifteen years with Metropolitan Insurance and a wife who ran off with the Jacuzzi salesman as if that was a big deal. I've got a B.A. in Accounting. I've got a house, two cars and a boat. I've got a wife and a kid and a whole collection of in-laws. They're all lined up on my dresser back home. Beside my sticker book and my flags of the world.

And you know what else? Ryan P. is a lard ass. You should see him. He's got three chins and legs the size of an elephant. Plus he's always shoving in front of me in the swing line. Then he hogs the swing. Even though he knows the rules: a turn is made up of twenty swings. A turn is ten swings one way, ten swings the other way. Then you get off. Like a civilized person. You get off. And if there's time, you go to the back of the line and start waiting all over again. Everyone knows this.

Except for Ryan P. He doesn't have a clue about anything. He says twenty swings is not enough to get your hair blowing. He says you can't even see China with twenty swings. Ryan P. is such an idiot, he takes as long as he likes at the swing. And nobody does a thing but get mad. When I scream at him to get off, when I throw rocks and junk at him, all he does is laugh and pump even higher.

"Take a hike dick-weed," he shouts in front of everyone. To me, a bookkeeper with the Federal government!

That's usually when all the pushing and arm twisting in the line-up starts, everybody being in such a bad mood by then because Ryan P. is refusing to follow the rules. That's why we hate him.

Elaine says we should waste him but I figure it's best to tell on him. That's what I'm doing right now. I'm saying all this stuff about Ryan P. so that everyone all the way to China will know what a pain he is and why he shouldn't be allowed.

One time I told on him to the yard supervisor, Ms. Tatlow, but it didn't do any good. She was wandering around the swing yard during one of our swing times. She had on these red high heels which made her about as tall as the top of the swing bar and I gave up my place in line to run up to her and tell her all about Ryan P. hogging the swing and how it wasn't fair and how Elaine only gave me so much allowance a week and it practically all went to belong to the Swing Club, the only place in a bizarre world where there was proper, organized swinging. I told her, too, how having my turn at swing was so important to me. How I counted on it after a horrible day of debits and credits in the city and how swinging had become the most important thing in my life next to my collection of sad ballads from the 19th century.

And you know what Ms. Tatlow did? She smiled. Then she took me by the shoulders right there in the swing yard and hugged me to her chest and whispered, "There, there Victor," and started putting her tongue in my ear and dragging me off towards her office and . . . well . . . afterwards she told me not to tell a single soul what we had done or she'd fix it so that I'd never swing again. So that's what happens when you tell someone in charge. You get it right in the ear.

I figure maybe if I make up a story about Ryan P. then everyone will know who he is and hate him too. This is what I'll say:

RYAN P. SUCKS DEAD BEARS!#*?

Then I'll save up for a billboard. I'll save up for a plane to trail a message. Or I'll print up a flyer to stick in the windshields at the Swing Club parking lot.

Elaine says, "Don't be insane." She says we should gang up on him. Or bribe him.

So maybe I'll try that now because I'm getting nervous standing here in the swing line. There's not much time left before dark and the Swing Club hasn't gone in for night lighting yet.

"Hey, Ryan P.!" I grab his three-piece Worsted at the shoulder. "You can have my whole collection of LaCoste shirts if you let me get ahead of you in the swing line."

He turns around sneering. "They wouldn't fit."

"You can have my very best sad ballad. You can have Barbara Allen."

Ryan P. just laughs. "Everyone knows, you moron, that sad ballads make your dick fall off."

Then suddenly he looks scared. "I gotta have that

swing," he says and goes charging off up the line, knocking guys out of the way, right and left.

So Ryan P.'s got the swing again and he's been up there for nearly two hours, the longest time he's ever hogged the swing. It's gotten dark and cold out and there's this mean November wind blowing the leaves off the trees and all us guys on the ground are getting frozen standing in line listening to Ryan P. yell, "I can just about see the lights of China!"

Not only that, but we're starting to get bored.

So it's a big relief when someone jumps out of the line ahead of me and shouts, "Hey, I know where there's this lady who eats penitentiaries!"

Now everyone is getting really excited about what this other guy has to say. And everyone is asking questions like how many penitentiaries can she eat at one time and what kind of penitentiaries she prefers, big ones or little ones, and if she eats the prisoners, too, and if so, what kinds of prisoners she likes best, bank robbers or murderers?

And this is giving me a new idea. Maybe we could get Ryan P. made into a prisoner on account of his always hogging the swing. Maybe there's a law against hoggers that I don't know about. And then maybe we could get him thrown into a penitentiary and have the lady who eats penitentiaries let loose on it. And, well, that would be the end of Ryan P. wouldn't it? I mean, nobody can ever escape from a penitentiary eater, can they? Not even Ryan P., that total gross nerd idiot with feet like a duck. Not even him.

PHILOSOPHER'S MIX

Sara J. must be ready for the nut house if she thinks I'm going to take one more midnight climb with her. I'm fed up with her promises. She just doesn't realize the difficulty and expense these climbs of hers are costing me.

There's the gas, for one. The price for gas for the car trip to her house before we can even begin the climb has become prohibitive; you don't get a mileage allowance when you're on a mission. Then there is the new husband to consider. Oh sure, he was supportive of my climbs in the beginning but lately he has been insisting that I stay home at nights with him and I am realizing that this is the right and natural thing to do.

Did I mention the sheer weariness of the effort? It takes me a full half hour to reach Sara J.'s house by car which means I must slip out of my warm bed by eleven o'clock at the latest. Add another half hour for finding a new steep hill since we can never climb the same steep hill twice—as a leader Sara J. is some tyrant—and then it's midnight and we haven't even started our climb which is another thing. Why midnight? What about this strange business of Sara J.'s of always having to climb steep hills at midnight? Why not on a Sunday afternoon when I could take the husband along? Why not, say, at ten in the morning when we could admire the view? And another thing, these climbs can often last most of the night. By morning I am completely exhausted, quite useless for ordinary living. And I won't even mention the bruises from struggling over the larger boulders, or the damp, or the wind.

It's too much.

I know. I know her rules. Sara J. has harangued me often enough with them: we must do our uphill toiling in the dark, as always; we must not be side-tracked by sensual delights (the husband); we must strive upwards in our search for the Final Ingredient which is to be found, Sara J. believes, at the end of one of our dark, uphill labours; we must strive upwards in our bare feet . . .

Bare feet? Something else about which Sara J. will not see reason, that ancient custom of the bare feet.

And now she is calling for a climb practically every

night. I say it has gone too far, my feet will not take it, I am not the young chicken I once was. Just because Sara J. is pregnant and fearful of losing ground due to the imminent birth of her child—a fact, which I am sure, will not deter her in her quest one bit—just because she believes that the Final Ingredient—the fuel from the tank of an Air East Jumbo Jet—is close at hand, just because she believes she will now, finally, be able to make the Philosopher's Mix . . .

Well, I for one, have had it. I've reached a decision. Sara J. can find herself a new follower. I'm going to send her a note. I'm going to tell her I'm through climbing steep hills at midnight. I'm going to tell her I don't believe any more in her Philosopher's Mix, nor do I have any faith in what it will produce in me when I drink it. Her vision of us one night sitting cross-legged on the asphalt and drinking the brew from the tea cups our mothers gave us on the occasion of our first menses no longer engages me. That bit about dangling our feet over the edge of infinity, transcendence finally in our possession, no longer inspires me.

Oh, I know what she'll say. She'll chide my flat, warm existence, she'll make fun of my new-found interest in the husband. But she's got to realize that not all of us can stay interested in climbing like she undoubtedly will. She's got to realize that some of us eventually like nothing better than a warm bed, a hand to hold and lots and lots of sleep.

MOUSE INCIDENT

I'm living in this here car crash. Everything else is at the shop. Ever since I gave the two mice back to their rightful owner, my former-former wants nothing to do with me. I ask you, two mice, he trashed me for two mice, is that right?

I live in this here car crash other side of the highway now. Not far from the hospital where I do volunteer work on my days off from the gift shop.

The last straw, he said.

I said, you didn't have to look after them, you didn't have the underfoot worry.

There we were, my girlfriends and I, out for a day in the country when we went into this roadside bar. Well, we were about to go in when this guy, looks like that TV actor sells insurance, he says, hey, are you wearing my hat?

Wearing your hat?

Yeah, wearing my hat.

I had on this green felt hat I'd found and it's where I kept the two mice when I went out of the house, tied to the brim. Weren't even my mice to begin with, I found them when I found the hat.

So this guy says, hey, that's my hat and my mice you're wearing, I'd know those two mice anywhere. And he says to the mice, Isn't that right babies? and kisses the brim of the hat.

Well, good God, I said, here, take them.

He was so grateful we all went into the bar to celebrate.

The names of my mice are Teresa Apollinaire and Sir Walter Martin, he told me, and anyone who goes to such trouble to name his mice, I thought, anyone who so obviously needs his mice, well, I never doubted they were his.

Here, I said, happily happily great relief and unleashing the mice from the hat, here take them, they're yours, and we all had another drink to celebrate the reunion.

So what happens next when I get home with no hat and no mice? My former-former goes nuts.

How could you give away my mice (*my mice!*) to a total stranger, he howls.

I said, He didn't look like a total stranger to me, he

looked like that actor sells insurance on TV and besides, they weren't even your mice to begin with, and anyone who goes to such trouble to name his mice when you didn't even bother and left me to do all the looking after, well.

Anything for a story, he says, you'll do anything for a story, well here's one, out you go.

That's why I'm living in this here car crash left up the highway some time ago now. Mangled home life, you might say. It's what I tell my young accident victims, the ones I volunteer to on my days off, the teenaged girls ending up in hospital from one thing or another.

Get the mangled part of your lives over with early, I tell them, clear the garbage out of the way now. Look at me, I'm thirty-five years old. Imagine spending thirty-five years working up to that one mouse incident.

My former-former, he says I've got no moral conscience, giving away those mice but I tell you, I got a letter from the true mouse owner thanking me. Now that he has Teresa and Sir Walter back, he says, things are going right in his life again: no more riding around in the rain with his convertible top down.

So I'm writing a story about that now, sitting in the scrunched front seat of my domicile car crash. I've got things to say about mouse incidents *in general*—hickory, dickory, docking away at our best intentions. The wreckage they can cause.

The clock struck one. Struck me.

Those mice, they weren't exactly children after all, they weren't exactly blind—just two small brown pet mice always underfoot and I gave them away and I'm glad.

And so I'm writing this story to you on a melting popsicle.

Melting popsicle? you say.

Yeah, melting popsicle.

Even now as I write—drip, drip, drip. But you're not minding, are you? Now that you think about it, you're not minding at all.

You like the way the black ink mingles with the pink popsicle then just soups away, a melting opus. You like the way these things, these opus things, slip stickily through our fingers, one minute a tick-tocking object so prettily formed, and the next, a dirty stain spreading on the car crash floor.

HAPPY BIRTHDAY

I asked my husband to hang from the bedroom window by his feet. Our window is quite high off the ground so there would be a certain amount of hazard involved in this gesture. I wanted a crowd gathering and, being in a hurry, having my husband hang from the window was the quickest way I could think of to achieve this end. I had in mind a silent, reflective crowd, rather subdued, no riotous interplay between crowd participants, none of that.

I hung my husband from our bedroom window head first, naked. The nakedness, a sure touch, I felt. I wanted a crowd gathered *wondering:* a throng of giant Shasta Daisies, their feathery heads turned upwards, swaying in the morning breeze. A gesture which would impress my neighbours with its originality.

For their part, my neighbours are an ordinary lot; on Mondays they string their husbands out on clotheslines and let them flap in a brisk wind; on Saturdays they paint them daffodil-yellow and plant them singly along the sidewalks of our street—stiff soldiers rat-a-tatting along as far as the eye can see. No crowd gatherings possible with these crude gestures.

As for myself, I will grasp at the inspired gesture wherever I can find it so don't give me a boring bouquet of husbands for my Happy Birthday or two dozen chocolate-covered husbands asleep in a red satin box, either. I wouldn't appreciate it.

THE TWO GENTLE LADIES FROM K-MART

I'm in the basement coffee room at K-Mart, the downtown store. I came in here looking for cheap dish towels and the two women in Household Items told me to wait in here, in their coffee room, a small, dingy room somewhere in the basement of the building.

There's some cold pizza in a box on the coffee table and they suggested that I might like to help myself to some or make myself some instant coffee if I get thirsty. Then they went away and locked the door.

I had a look at the pizza but declined a slice. With curling bits of dry salami sprinkled over its surface it hardly looked appetizing.

For some reason the K-Mart ladies think I am wonderful. Every now and then they peek in at me to show me to the other sales ladies from Home Furnishings and Lingerie. Giggling together, they are extremely polite and deferential and all agree that I am quite a find.

But I can't understand why they regard me as some kind of marvellous jewel they have just discovered or happened upon, so marvellous they wish to keep me here for their own private viewing.

Still, they are trying to keep me happy—I can't fault them for that—by telling me they've got an especially good bargain in dish towels (just for me!) and they're arranging the items upstairs, this very minute, stapling them all together and sticking on the price tags. All marked down to one cent apiece. A bargain indeed. So I am grateful for their endeavours on my behalf and hesitate to protest my capture. Because that is what it is. A capture and imprisonment of sorts although I am sure the two gentle ladies from K-Mart wouldn't call it that. They would be offended if I were to suggest it. To them I am merely a tempting, interesting specimen they found to ferret away and marvel at during their coffee breaks.

All well and good. I hate to disappoint them but my wife is waiting for me in front of the Bank of Commerce on the corner of Yates and Douglas. I told her I wouldn't be long—just stopping in at K-Mart to pick up some dish towels, I said—and knowing her, she's still standing there, out front of the bank. She will wait all day and longer if I ask her to and I worry because she doesn't know how to wait correctly. That is, without drawing attention to herself. Anonymously. She will wait rather too far out on the sidewalk, for instance, so that she becomes like an island in the pedestrian flow that people must break apart and steer around.

The other problem is that she twirls. She's an expert on twirling, on her heel and bending down. Sometimes she can manage two, three, twirls at one go. This is fine for our backyard barbecues but suicide on a busy street.

So I really am worried for her. But what can I do, trapped as I am like some fabulous insect? The K-Mart ladies seem to regard me as a model house-husband which I certainly am not. It's just that I like a bargain. It would be all right if they took me for an ideal shopper, though, because there could be some commercial advantage in that. I could have my picture taken and appear on their advertising flyers drying dishes with my new dish towels. For a small fee, of course, there's no denying I could use the cash. But no, the K-Mart ladies prefer to keep me for themselves, a found object, somehow giving meaning to their daily work at the store. Meanwhile I worry about my wife.

There's a small window near the ceiling of the coffee room. By climbing up onto the coffee table I can see the church across the street and for the past while I have been occupying myself by drawing a likeness of this church in the lined notebook I always carry with me. It's a large church, resembling three same-sized blocks with a stick on top, quite simple to draw.

When the K-Mart ladies peek in on their next coffee break, they are disappointed that I have not eaten a slice of their cold pizza, so to accommodate them, because they really are very nice ladies, I summon my courage and eat a piece. This pleases them so much that I am encouraged and show them my rather crude drawing of the church, torn hastily from my notebook. They take it solemnly, with tears in their eyes, and study it appreciatively. What do they see there, I wonder? But before another moment has passed they hand me a set of bargain dish towels (at no charge), unlock the door and wave me farewell. (But keeping the picture, I might add, for themselves.)

Now I am free to go and have hurried off in search of my wife.

I find her standing in front of the bank, too far out from the curb and twirling, as I had feared, drawing angry stares from the passing crowds.

So I have taken her now by the arm and together we are hurrying up Yates Street. Correctly, on the right side of the sidewalk, because in this life the journey is perilous enough—what with the chance imprisonments that can befall you at any moment—without inviting further misery by disobeying the rules of the road as well.

SAUCERS

I *mixed the salad with the chili making one sloppy mess hoping that would allow the food to go further. Added sawdust, too, and water, leaves, a few stones, never expecting to feed so many. Found a can of dog food left over from when we had the dog, so added that. Plus crackers, popcorn, a dash of dish soap to make it froth and called it hearty stew. This stew-like mush not smelling too bad, all masked by the hot chili flavor. A hasty dinner thrown together for the guests; they would show up uninvited. Luckily there were buns in the freezer and buns can always stretch a meal. I served the food on tea cup saucers, a frozen bun at saucer's edge, then arranged the saucers on a silver tray to take to the guests told to wait outside. They were packed together by the good neighbour fence and growling like dogs at the unknown. I was hoping my stew would quieten their noise. It's terrible the demands guests will make.*

ETIQUETTE

for Pauline Holdstock

I. DINNER PARTIES

I was telling you how I put the strips of bloody steak into the dryer to dry them out before serving the guests and you said you wished Barbara Harris had done something like that the night before because Barbara Harris had cooked the bacon with the ham, had layered it, so that when you cut into your piece of ham it wasn't cooked. It was, in fact, white inside. *Oh look* you said *my piece of ham is white.* And neither Barbara Harris nor her husband Howard Harris said a word but went right on eating. Then a few minutes later Barbara Harris hissed across the table to her husband *I told you it wouldn't work cooking them together like that* and Howard Harris hissed back *Fuck off* and the whole dinner took on an aspect of terror. So then we wondered what was the right thing to do in a situation like that, what would Emily Post have said if your host tells your hostess to fuck off in the middle of the meal? How do you repair the collapse of a social situation and should you even want to? It wasn't as if Barbara Harris and her husband were family or really good friends and you could say *lighten up* or *knock it off* to them like you would to your kids, tell them to go to their rooms and don't come back until they've sorted things out or don't come back at all. I mean the whole idea of dining with friends or, in this case, the casually known, is to get away from stew pot situations like that and grab for yourself a fistful of peace away from the fray. But Emily Post came up short. She was fixated on knives and forks, introductions and thank-you notes. She didn't in all her one thousand pages even have a sentence about fuck-off situations at dinner. And so I was wondering if the time hadn't come for a few good words to be said about the etiquette that lurks beneath the surface of manners. Since everyone is going on about subtexts these days, it's clear there's a subtext of manners and perhaps it's time to re-organize the laws of etiquette along dadaist lines. I mean, put the knives and forks back on the ceiling where they belong and decorate the table with fuck-offs or fuck-ups depending on the course. And in the case of Barbara Harris and her husband, the thing to do would be to stuff them into your going-out-to-dinner hand bag and take them home to the dog or throw them into tomorrow's soup. They'd make a good base. They might even make a really interesting soup depending on how much meat was on their bones and so the whole family could salvage nourishment from a fuck-off situation. And somehow this solution is the right thing to do with the Harris' hissing away together in the soup pot, somehow this makes us feel pleased with the world.

2. CLEANING THE KITCHEN

You were in a good mood and said it was because this was the first time in six weeks that you'd cleaned the kitchen and how cleaning the kitchen always made the kids happy. We were having coffee at the unusually clear table and the kids, all four of them, were hanging about, one on your lap, the others on the floor at our feet leaning against our ankles with sweet solemn smiles on their faces. Not doing anything, just being calm in the clean kitchen. Everything was ordered and neat for a change while chaos had been banished to outside the kitchen window after a long six-week struggle to disorder the room. *I gave chaos a rest* you said *it just gets worn out from all the work it has to do around here.* And we looked outside to where chaos had gathered itself all grey and shapeless against the window pane. Then one of the kids sighed from looking at it, then another, then another, until you took pity and said *Ah go let it in.* So the littlest kid ran to open the kitchen door and it didn't take a moment for a sudden gust of wind to scatter a thousand leaves over the newly washed floor and to blow a sheaf of papers off a shelf. Then for no reason one of the kids bit his own tongue and howled and another suddenly whined for food. And getting up to go I knocked over my cup of coffee. Then the dog got stepped on and started barking. And the telephone rang and the front doorbell rang and all the kids ran from the room to see who was there knocking over one chair two chairs as they tracked through the spilt coffee. *Welcome home* you said to chaos who by now had settled by the stove and was busy causing a pot of oatmeal to boil over.

3. THEME PARTIES

Everyone was having theme parties. The most popular were toga parties where fat businessmen got to dress up in sheets and their wives put on Cleopatra eyes though they were really copying Liz Taylor in the movie. Everyone had seen *Animal House* and liked the grossness of John Belushi farting and puking and grabbing tits so some of that was okay in the lovely living rooms of friends. We went as master and slave, something different we thought, you as the slave attached to a twenty-foot length of rope, a dog collar around your neck and wearing a burlap toga. For a laugh we went to the door, me first, and I said *Daddy can't make it this evening so I brought a friend* then tugged on the rope and you appeared from behind a rhododendron bush dragging your leg late-nite-monster-style and grunting like a wild man. We went into the living room like that, amongst the thirty or so be-sheeted guests drinking white wine and eating broccoli spears and I said to you loudly *Go lie down over there by the couch.* And you did and it was really weird because the room got quiet and stayed that way the whole half hour you kept up the slave thing, grunting and grabbing anyone who got near 'til I took you a beer signalling the show was over. But the rest of the night we might have been lepers. Trying to talk gardening or falling interest rates got us nowhere. So here's another example of etiquette and what not to do at theme parties. Find out first what the script is and never never deviate from it. Do something acceptable like drive a Harley through the front door or toss the veggie plate through the living room window or go fornicate with a neighbour on the basement stairs or just stay home.

4. ENDANGERED OBJECTS

Another example of etiquette concerns the strange invitation we got. It had so many words at first I thought it was a chain letter threatening good luck. But, no, it was an invitation for a time-out party, the words explaining how everyone these days had enviro-fatigue from trying to do the right thing by the environment, how all that garbage-sorting, healthful-living business was wearing everyone out. Not to mention the private hand-wringing going on about depleting rain forests, fish, bird, bear, and whale stocks as if the whole horrible state of things came down to each person alone, some huge accusing finger pointing at them: THIS LATE 20TH CENTURY MESS IS YOUR FAULT. So the invitation had the time-out sign printed in amongst the words, the T made with the hands, and listed a bunch of party rules such as bring your own styrofoam cup, a really shocking suggestion since we always carry our pottery mugs everywhere like good kids. Rule number two was bring a can of aerosol something—hairspray, deodorant, air freshener—take your pick. These items would be raffled off, the idea being they were endangered objects, would probably be worth mega bucks in years to come. The next rule was wear something plastic, a garbage bag cape, say, or an asphalt bra. Then the invitation said how entertainment was being planned: a really good stand-up comic was all set to tell hilarious jokes about toxic waste. And there would be door prizes, too—a case of aspartame, a case of diazinon. The food, of course, would be processed and served dead in colourful boxes. But the party's highlight would be a fifteen-foot-high bonfire made up of bread bags and rigid plastic containers which would be lit at midnight and we would all be expected to dance around it holding hands while the media filmed us. They were guaranteed to show up late like important guests, an entire fleet of TV vans sprinkled with obsolete computer chips like sharp confetti. But I didn't know whether I should attend this spectacular event or even the proper way to answer the invitation since there was no r.s.v.p. No word, either, about whether to bring a bottle of wine or a vegetable tray and nothing in any of the etiquette books made any sense when it came to time-out parties. So what I did was copy most of the invitation here and I'm passing it along hoping at least twenty people will read it and get good luck. I heard a family of four from Elbow, Saskatchewan were saved from an encounter with a marauding cloud of radon gas because they stayed inside reading this piece. I heard a guy in Des Moines, Iowa was struck by insight after reading this piece. I heard that if you don't pass this piece along to twenty of your friends then all the wonderful things that were supposed to happen to you in your life could very likely go up in a puff of toxic smoke.

SCORE

My husband of eighteen years announced he was going back to his first wife. He'd been married to her for two years twenty years ago and brought many stories of hating her to our marriage. I loved those stories. One time she flung herself screaming onto the hood of his car. Once, in a fit of anger, she smashed his tropical fish tank. Fifteen Siamese Fighting Fish, seven Zebras, two Tri-coloured Sharks gasping for air on the wall-to-wall Berber.

But your first wife? I asked him. Why?

Real estate, he said.

The first wife might be part of our family's history but

I wasn't eager for her to take over the here and now. Our kids called her Boo Boo. I called her Boo Hoo, though her real name was Charlene. She was famous for crying.

Tell me again, I said. Why real estate?

She makes a lot of money, my husband said. I tried a thing or two to change his mind. While I might not be making bags of money thinking about this wily world, I do on occasion write a clever story. I tried sitting at my desk naked from the waist down, pencil in hand. No interest. I invented some zappy Erma Bombeck thoughts, put them inside a cartoon bubble and attached the bubble to his mind on a string. Ho hum.

I tried keeping score for him. I kept score anywhere I could. On the fridge door in black marker I wrote: My Life 18 - Her Life 2. He didn't find it funny. I arranged his Cheerios on a plate to read: Dead Tropical Fish 24 - Current Live Household Pets 4. On his Father's Day wrapping paper I scrawled: Our Children 2 - Her Children 0. But his heart was thrusting elsewhere.

Tell us about the time crazy old Boo Boo stayed in the cherry tree for three days and cried because you forgot her birthday. This from our youngest. Tell us about the time she slugged you in the bar. The time she spiked your tea with Ex-Lax. The time she went on your job interview and did all the talking to make sure you got the job. Stories better than Archie. I saw my mistake. On the front door with red crayon I wrote: Boo Hoo Nostalgia Tales 23 - Resident Adult Female's Neo-Neurotic Tales of Life & Laughter 5,292.

Then I cleaned the fridge. My husband said, Twice in eighteen years is not a good score. Our son said, It looks like you won't be making it to the play-offs.

As a tribute to the extra mile I was running on behalf of the family, I abandoned books on philosophy and took up a new kind of reading. I got a book on dances; I'd heard it takes two to tango. A book on archaeology, leaving no stone unturned. A book about growing grass over the septic tank, with special instructions for laughing at all costs. I was looking for a doorway into not caring.

Finally I asked my husband that pearl of a question: what can she give you that I . . . ?

Small kitchen appliances, he said, then listed them off: an electric popcorn maker, a toaster oven, an ice-cream machine, three different models of blender, a food processor, an electric can opener, an electric knife, a hand-held electric mixer, an old-fashioned electric mixer with three sizes of bowls that fit into each other, a yoghurt maker, an electric juicer, a bread maker, five different kinds of coffee makers, a singing kettle, an electric kettle, a small microwave oven for the family room.

Big deal, I said. What else?

History, he said, getting to the science of the matter.

History? I asked. What about the time she cleaned up

in the divorce settlement? Remember what a maniac she was? All you got was the idiot dog and the hat stand.

Exactly, he said. Once-upon-a-time. I'm sick of the present.

You want history? I said. Well, remember this. Then I burned down the house.

Standing before the charred and smoking elbows of two-by-fours which had once been our three bedroom split level on a quiet cul-de-sac, my husband looked at me with new interest.

Our son said, Remember the time Mom burned down the house because Dad was going back to Boo Boo. Even though it happened only an hour ago. Our daughter said, I loved it when Mom had all that ash on her face. She looked like something out of *Star Wars.* There was pride in their voices.

My husband said, Okay, you win. I'll settle for a two-hole toaster with a special slot for toasting English muffins.

We moved into a motel. Our son hung a victory banner over the doorway to room 203. It read: HISTORY RULES.

For a while I didn't mind running the history-making department; I believed it was my duty as a parent, as a fully participating member of the community. And, I reasoned, when you've got history you've got time at your back—it doesn't get a chance to overtake you. You can sit on a lawn chair and not worry about time passing you by. You can dangle your feet over the edge of your existence, lean on fence posts if you can find one, drum your fingers monotonously on cardboard tables. I can see the sense of this, the beauty of this. But there's history and there's history.

I packed my bags and moved next door to room 205. A day later I heard our daughter say, remember the time Mom said that history is a whole world of meanings and not just memorable events strung out in a hopscotch line? I liked it when she climbed onto the motel roof with the megaphone, the way the crowd gathered like a threatening storm, and the firemen and the sirens.

I had done none of these things. It looked like my daughter was well on her way to creating a remember-the-time world of her own.

But my husband?

I called up Boo Hoo. He's all yours, I told her.

Who? she said. Never heard of him.

THE STEPMOTHER AND THE UGLY DAUGHTERS

The English family who rents out our living room and master bedroom is always complaining about something. This morning it was the view from the living room window.

Too North American, they said.

Objecting to the eight-lane freeway and billboard display. So I bought two shades of green paint and painted a pastoral scene on the plate glass window.

Upsetting the female gym teachers who occupy our second and third bedrooms.

You're giving the English family preference, they said, and demanded full use of the hallway. For their exercise equipment—bench press, stationary bike, swing.

And as might be expected, the pensioner in the half-bathroom began whining. This time, kitchen privileges.

It's not easy plugging a hot plate into an electric razor outlet, she said.

So I let her use the kitchen for thirty minutes at four. Even though the kitchen is where I live with my new husband and his two robust daughters.

Now the word is out.

The taxi driver who camps on our front porch steps has summoned up his courage.

It's only fair, he says. Flinging open the kitchen cupboards, helping himself to the canned goods.

My new husband is at the kitchen sink washing dishes. He wants nothing to do with the tenants. Renting out was my idea. To make extra money for the boarding school fees. In six months I should have saved up enough to get rid of the daughters for good.

But I worry they might not go.

They follow us everywhere like two spoiled dogs. They even followed us on our honeymoon to Lake Louise. Managing to steal an old twelve-footer to slap in the water alongside us while we tried to find peace in our canoe. Laughing at our nakedness. Growling, snapping at our nakedness.

They're ugly daughters with fine black moustaches and they're lounging now on their camp cots over by the walk-in-pantry. They haven't even noticed the manic-depressive who's just charged through the door. He uses the laundry room on Tuesdays and Fridays.

What have you done with the Pine-Sol? he shrieks at them, pacing the room in a frenzy.

But the daughters ignore him. Instead they sneer at me.

We know what you're up to and it'll take more than a crowbar to get rid of us, they say.

Patting Wolf, the stray Pit Bull, who lives at the foot of their cots.

The stepmother and the ugly daughters, it's an old, old story and we're not worried, they say. You can rent out the house from here to forever, we know what's in store for you, they say.

CHILDLESS

They all want to be our child. They are lining up on the patio, all manner of them wanting to be our child. Bouquets of red heads, small dainty boys. The girls are putting on wigs and doing dances. The boys are spinning in circles until they faint. All day long they call to me, "Play something on the piano," and hand me sheet music through the open living room window. I am obliging. I play something of Beethoven's or a lively Irish jig. Then they do cartwheels on our front lawn hoping I'll notice and pick the best one. When the telephone rings they rush in clamouring to answer it. The lucky one laughing gets to say, "It's for you Mommy." I can't decide. I can't decide which one to take. They do not have names yet, these children. My husband will be home soon. I have to pick a child before he comes home. One child. He's out taking pictures of Captains for his scrap book. All day long he roams the docks, snapping. As long as he can find a new Captain to snap he's happy. It doesn't matter what kind of boat the Captain is in charge of although he prefers submarines. My husband has agreed reluctantly that I can pick one child. I've got to decide by suppertime. My husband is so particular. What if he doesn't like my choice? All the children are adorable. There's a tiny girl doing somersaults outside my window. A tiny girl. There's a twelve-year-old boy sitting in a row boat on our front lawn—no water. Just sitting in the boat gazing out upon the wide suburban sea. My husband would like him, I know. He could make the boy Captain of the row boat. They could spend many happy hours together, snapping. Perhaps my husband will reconsider and allow me to pick two children, one each, and I could have the tiny red-wigged girl. All day long I could sit at the piano playing *Fur Elise* while she dressed in feathers and net could perform cart-wheels, handsprings on my living room carpet calling out to me over and over with her sweet tiny voice, "Mommy Mommy watch me do this." I've got to decide by suppertime. My husband will be home then. It's my only chance.

THE LOCAL WOMEN ARE PERFORMING A TRADITIONAL DANCE

The local women are performing a traditional dance. Twelve of them have lined up in the parking lot outside Save-On-Foods wearing their special costumes—a loose fitting garment made of a flowered cotton material called a *house dress.* Around their waist is tied the ceremonial *apron*, a square of material, also of cotton, which hangs in front of their bodies to protect the *house dress* from soap suds, grease stains, the muddy hands of grasping children. Usually the *apron* is solid white in colour but it may be pastel or checked and sometimes it has pockets or a ruffle around the edge. It all depends on which locale the women are from. Urban women are known for canvas *aprons* in solid colours, women of the suburbs, for nostalgia *aprons* trimmed with lace. Pay close attention: the *apron* of former times was used (metaphorically) to tie the women to something called *domesticity*, a state of hominess created by them for men and for children.

The dancing women wear dark red lipstick, their faces are smudged with pastry flour and from their hands swing *cast iron frying pans.* On their feet are the authentic *fuzzy pink slippers* of the dance and though difficult to imagine, these slippers have been solemnly passed down from one generation of dancer to the next. They are made of acrylic—a petroleum by-product which will last forever. The dancers' heads are covered with *curlers*, three-inch metal tubes around which strands of hair are wound and affixed to the head with steel pins called *bobby pins.* These *curlers* complete the traditional dress.

Now watch as the women dance. Those strings of single family dwellings, plastic laundry baskets, dogs, cats, sectional sofas, and six-month-old babies which are attached to the yellow polypropylene cord trailing from their right ankles are called *domestic paraphernalia.* They form part of the complicated twirling and hopping movement of the dance. Each dancer must spin in a circle, moving at such a rate as to lift the cord off the ground. She will then hop over the spinning cord at least once with each rotation. Two hops is sensational. Three—nothing less than sublime.

The more *domestic paraphernalia* trailing from the right leg of a dancer, the more prestige a dancer will have. This is because a long, heavy line of goods will be harder to spin and hop over than a shorter one. Fatigue is a problem, as is tripping because as the dancer spins she must jump higher and higher. Only the best dancers can sustain the dance.

The traditional dance of women is a frantic dance and the accompanying music must reflect this frenzy. Circus music meant for jugglers and acrobats is good. A hurried up version of *Entrance of the Gladiators* or *The Flight of the Bumble Bee* is also used. *So is The One-Minute Symphony*—repeated endlessly.

Now you know why the women's traditional dance is performed in an empty parking lot—the hazard factor—the essential ingredient of all good dances, that brush with death. Any minute now a house could be loosened from the strings of *domestic paraphernalia* and be hurled into the spectators. Hence the expression *raining cats and dogs.* So stand back. As a member of the crowd you've got to be careful, keep your head down, and be aware of the exits.

When the women perform their traditional dance the effect can be quite dizzying. Twirling, stomping, shouting, the momentum quickens, the paraphernalia spins. Whole city blocks have been toppled by flying debris. Sometimes the dancers themselves take flight, riding their washing machines and garbage cans high over the heads of the gasping spectators. Once Delores Delmonte, that famous, furious solo dancer, unleashed a shopping mall. A terrible, wonderful sight.

This group we're watching now is particularly fine, especially that woman, third from the left, the one in the pink-and-blue-check *house dress.* She's managed to string a good six hundred meters of domesticity behind her. Even a small bank—no wait, there's more. Several institutions as well—a hospital, a school, a television station. My god, she's spinning her cord two feet off the ground. An inspiration! And her jumps! Look at those jumps. Two! Three! There's a fourth! And she's still upright. Incredible. But hold on. That school is coming loose. There it goes, yes, it's beginning to rise. A magnificent ascent.

And those children. Look what's happening to those children: shaken from their classrooms along with their desks, books, blackboards, teachers. Sprinkling over the crowd like confetti.

Bravo!

Bravo!

STEEL BLANKET

We listened peacefully to the archangel singing and he told us that within this day fossils would be found belonging to a former fabulous beast but that no one would care. Who cares for fabulous beasts these days? he said, when it's all pull and carry the load and nothing of sweet surrender beneath the trees. I wondered if the archangel cared at all for our present toiling; there's not a day I'm without worry. There's costs to be met in back alleyways and exchanges to take place and all of this is riotous to the soul which longs for something else. The alternatives are hidden like nasty secrets beneath a steel blanket. I'm sorry to have to say this but the very factories are run one piece at a time and with no bother for the ordinary man toiling under metal skies. Even now the freeway is filled with sleepers. I'm sorry to have to say this but those responsible for fire must always do the burning. Just as those of us who venture beyond the walls in search of the fabulous beast often return afraid, becoming like disturbed children confined to our rooms for pain.

RAW MATERIAL

Go feed Daddy," I said to my daughter Janice.

Needing something special from him, I had prepared a tray of cheeseburgers and french fries for his lunch.

Janice whined as usual—you know what nine-year-olds are like—but I said (again) that if she didn't take her responsibilities seriously then what kind of adult would she grow into?

"You have two choices," I told her, "you can either feed Daddy or you can spend the rest of your life being gnawed at by the horrible guilt which will be your due and from which there is no escape."

She fed Daddy, grumbling, mind you, but grumbling I

can stand as long as they make the right decision. You can never let up with children, you must always be rigidly predictable in your responses to them. Some day I will write a book about this; child rearing is so obvious it hurts.

Janice reported back that Daddy liked his lunch but had smeared it all over his face again and that when she didn't laugh at his joke he got upset and started spitting at her.

Not for the first time did it occur to me that much of child rearing is like dog obedience: rules and expectations must be ruthlessly repeated, a monotonous chore to be sure, but so necessary in the proper handling of nine year olds, who are strange creatures at best—as Janice is, mostly teeth and argument and entirely without style: baseball hat, party dress, gum boots.

"Your father-daughter relationship will suffer needlessly if you fail to laugh at Daddy's jokes," I told her (again), "which means that you're going to have to clean him up or we'll never get any work done this afternoon and I'm beginning to feel desperate for a fresh idea."

We headed off towards the study at the other end of the rancher; already we could hear Daddy's shouting as he banged at his cage.

Janice kept up her toneless chatter all the while needing eye-contact and "uh-huh" from me at regular intervals. She was saying something about not having adequate peer relationships because of all the time she had to spend assisting Daddy and what kind of learning experience was it anyway if all she ever got to do was clean his cage or run the video equipment?

"I can see how you might feel," I told her. (You've got to give them some expression or they will turn into teenage time bombs.)

"However," I added, "you will soon be entering pre-adolescence and that is the time when you must start to emancipate your ego from the solipsistic concerns that now absorb you and begin to consider the welfare of the world at large. In your case, this will take the form of service to Art."

Janice replied snottily with something about my stage of life being an impossible one and that when she has children of her own she will never make them serve Art no matter how creatively important it is.

Fortunately her nattering stopped when we reached Daddy and his cage.

"Oh dear," I said when I saw him.

He was in his usual place, all right, bouncing on the recliner rocker that sat in the centre of the cage, but he had smeared ketchup and mustard all over his handsome face and several bread-and-butter pickles sat atop his head.

Janice smirked nastily, a gesture that seemed to be directed at me.

"Laugh now," I said, "but where was your laughter when it was needed?" There are times when I forget that I love Janice.

She got the pail and wash cloth and I unlocked the cage

door. It isn't a lot of work for her, the washing of Daddy's face and tidying his cage, but enough to warrant her two-dollar-a-week allowance. Children must learn the value of money and this is why I insist that Janice save at least half of her weekly allowance for something worthwhile. I believe she's saving up for an elephant.

Daddy doesn't mind having Janice in his cage. In fact, there are times when it seems he prefers playing Crazy Eights with her to having his weekly conjugal visit from me. He reassures me, though, that his card playing with Janice is important to him, a welcome respite from the vigorous demands that my creativity places upon him. All told, we three are a happy family and this is not often the case with families who serve Art.

But it was time for me to be stern with Daddy: this food on the face routine had been hilarious six weeks back but he had been doing it every day since and it was becoming downright stale. What's the point, I reasoned, of caging up your inspiration if all it yielded was stuck records? His original action, certainly, had resulted in quite a lively story, an apt metaphor for our materialistic times, and I had been screamingly pleased with Daddy then for suggesting it but now it was time for some fresh material.

Janice, I noticed, had now changed into her visor and she and Daddy were facing each other sitting cross-legged on the cage floor in preparation for a game of cards. Janice was dealing.

"Daddy," I whispered through the bars, "you're going to have to come up with something new. I need a new line, something unexpected. A brand new angle. I'm running out of raw material."

Daddy put down his cards and, sighing, pushed at the stacks of postmodern fiction that littered the cage. I was beginning to wonder if he ever read the stuff.

"Is there anything left over from your days at the steel mill that I haven't used?" I prompted. "Some funny little thing you used to do? Some quirky little thought you used to have?"

He shook his head morosely, picked up a copy of the *New York Times Review of Books* and softly tore at its pages. I could see that he was feeling his failure.

I motioned for Janice to absent herself from the cage. Nine-year-olds do not understand nuance: you have to spell out everything for them.

"Did you look at that piece on popular culture?" I asked. "Or that new theory of Disengagement that was highlighted in *Scientific American*?"

Daddy grunted.

"Nothing?"

Daddy grunted again.

"What about vanishing grizzly bears? The nuclear threat?" I cried, exasperation setting in. "Have you not had any dreams? Is there nothing left for me to use?"

What if my inspiration is drying up? I thought with

alarm. What if Daddy never yields another gem and our family business has to shut down? No more making of important fiction? Bankrupt Art? What if I have to change careers in mid-story?

Janice, meanwhile, had climbed out the study window.

Let her go, I thought. As a parent you should never take out your personal frustrations on your child; who knows what abnormal psychology they might indulge in, later on, if you do.

I had, of course, seen it coming. Daddy's off-the-wall comments, his bizarre antics (all those videos!) had become less and less frequent this past while. I had produced three volumes of short fiction based upon the inspiration I received from Daddy, but perhaps now he had nothing new to give me.

Janice climbed back in the window, pulling the garden hose behind her.

"What on earth?" I started to say just as she activated the nozzle.

A terrific gush, a quelling protester sort of gush, sprayed Daddy, the cage, the books, papers, myself.

Janice of the crazed eye manoeuvred behind the hose, all teeth and elbows, laughing, laughing maniacally.

"God is deader than thou!" she screamed.

Daddy and I, amidst the hosing, exchanged glances. "God is deader than thou!" Say it again Janice. "God is deader than thou!"

An interesting indictment. Existential possibilities. (Juices flowing.) Children's literature? An epic poem?

But that's the joy of child rearing, I reflected, as Daddy and I wrestled the hose from Janice and locked her in the cage: you never know what they will come up with next. Fresh ideas! New angles! So important not to stifle their creative urges, to keep their little minds ticking over with wonder, excitement, awe. (Is there something to be done with elephants?)

Children have a crucial role to play in the service of Art. I've often said it's the handling that counts, it all comes down to providing them with a proper home environment: nourishing food, clear guidelines and a healthy respect for their place in the untoward scheme of things.

FREE ENTERPRISE

The Businessmen are too hot and so they cannot eat. In the banquet room the tables are piled high with baked hams, chicken, beef. The Businessmen lie before the tables on yellow canvas lawn chairs with cool terry cloths draped over their eyes. Middle-aged serving women dressed as Harem slaves guard the entrance way to the room while the food on the tables slowly rots. The summer heat in the building is stifling; the air conditioning has not worked for several days. Everywhere there's the smell of garbage.

It drifts down the hallway to the Meeting Room where the Mayor and her Aldermen are debating what to do with the public money: programs for the poor or new landscaping for city hall? It's a short debate: landscaping wins. Two Aldermen drop dead in a fit of conscience.

The burly male secretary removes the bodies. Perspiring heavily, he drags the dead Aldermen by the feet to the outside hallway. First one, then the other. The Mayor calls out, "If they can't stand the heat they should stay out of the kitchen!" The surviving Aldermen laugh nervously. Meanwhile, the male secretary is perplexed: what do you do with two dead Aldermen?

He takes them to the Real Estate office on the second floor. Because the elevator is out of order, he drags the Aldermen up the back stairs and deposits them at the foot of the Receptionist's desk. She's confused and asks a passing Real Estate Agent what to do. Annoyed, the Agent says he's too busy to think, he's got an important ad to compose for a cute fixer-upper, don't bother him, deadlines are deadly.

The Receptionist and the male secretary position the bodies against the office wall and place FOR SALE signs around their necks. Then they depart to the Coffee Room where they spend their lunch hour in robust nakedness rolling around on melting blocks of ice and assuring one another that they have indeed found happiness on this earth.

Their happiness disturbs the Office Manager of the paving company next door who is already in a bad mood. She's too hot. The air conditioner has not worked in living memory and the smell of garbage is giving her a headache.

Mr. Sturgeon, her Accounts Receivable clerk, crouches beneath his desk. The Office Manager isn't pleased with Mr. Sturgeon, either; he hasn't been showing the proper enthusiasm towards his work. Consequently, she's had to attach his leg to the wall using a twenty-foot length of chain. The chain is long enough to allow Mr. Sturgeon to reach the bathroom or the Accounts Receivable filling cabinet should he feel inspired.

The Office Manager shouts, "That invoice for 47½ tonnes of hot mix asphalt has not been collected, has it, Mr. Sturgeon?"

Mr. Sturgeon whimpers.

She throws him a sixty-day account. There is some drooling on the part of Mr. Sturgeon. This encourages the Office Manager and she changes into her black lace and boots number with the matching whip. She runs a no-nonsense office.

Her efficiency, however, doesn't reach the top floor where the bankrupt owner of an office supply company crouches on the carpet of his empty, liquidated office. Naked, he is staring intently at the beige touch-tone telephone before him, yearning for deliverance from financial doom with an order for twenty thousand memo pads. Every nerve, every hair on his body strains, waiting for the telephone to ring. When it suddenly does ring, he grabs the receiver and, panting like a dog, holds it at his side for exactly ten seconds before replacing it to begin the manoeuvre again.

At nightfall, after the building's occupants have gone home, I, along with the legion of poor, come in to clean. We use cans of aerosol spray to subdue the smell of garbage. But it's too hot. Too hot to work. Instead we ransack the wastepaper baskets for useful supplies of paper-clips, pink slips, styrofoam cups. In the Banquet Room we line up respectfully before the heaped tables and help ourselves to the rotting food. Plates of decaying salmon, crab, veal and everything bathed in a rich cream sauce.

With my plate of food I stand at a second-story window and gaze out across the still warm city to the mercury vapour lights twinkling prettily in the distance. I consider how like a disastrous plane trip is our violent quest to get ahead: many will die, few will be saved in the endeavour.

Still, as a newly-hired cleaning woman, I am grateful for this opportunity to work and to feed from the rich man's coffers. In a fit of free enterprise I make plans for my sudden future: at the end of my shift I will drag the two dead Aldermen, first one, then the other below to the car park and there, in brisk subterranean trade, sell their bodies for parts.

STUDIES SHOW/ EXPERTS SAY

How much butylated hydroxalade does it take to make one mutant cell?" This is the question I pose to Isobel over dinner. "One millilitre? A quarter of a teaspoon?"

"Why don't you just shoot yourself and be done with it?" Isobel screams as she packs her bags. "I'm leaving you. Sicko. Pea brain. Bag of shit. You've got gas up the ass. And I'm taking the antibiotics with me."

"You'll be sorry," I tell her. "Studies show that being cut off from friendships and family doubles a person's chance of sickness and death. Not only that," I call from my sick bed, "but Experts say it is not enough to marry someone because they make your heart pound, two people's lifestyles must come together as well. What's a nurse without a patient?"

The main thing that worries me about living alone is this: what if I should stop breathing in my sleep? Sleep Apnoea. What if no one is there wake me, shake my shoulder or, if necessary, administer mouth to mouth? What if I am found dead in my bed, a rotting cauliflower, one ghastly hand still clutching my Merck's Manual of Diseases?

For this reason I call up Georgina, single mother of two, my client-girlfriend from the Welfare Office.

I say, "About forty percent of women who separated while still in their thirties will never re-marry. Now's your chance."

The chest pains start on the first Sunday after Georgina moves in. We send the kids to McDonald's and spend the rest of the afternoon in Emergency. I tell them this is my fifteenth heart attack.

"Skinny guys don't get heart attacks," the intern says. "It's probably just gas."

Driving home I say to Georgina, "What does the medical profession know? They've yet to discover why I am dying."

"Everyone dies," says Georgina. "In fact the outer limit of the human life-span remains at about 110 years and that figure hasn't changed since the beginning of recorded history."

"But you're not supposed to die in the prime of your life," I yell. "Not when you're a 42-year-old, white-collar Welfare Worker, three-bedroom home-owner secure in the middle-income profile bracket."

"You worry too much," says Georgina. "Worry wart! Next you'll be getting Herpes." Georgina is laughing.

"Very funny," I say. "Right now I'd be more worried about this pain in my lower right quadrant. I think I have a fever."

"Show me where it hurts," she says, unzipping my pants as I'm driving.

I pull over. She does the rebound test for Peritonitis, the way I taught her on our first night together. Nothing.

"Probably just a gas bubble," she says, hiking up her skirt and getting comfy.

Georgina lasted three weeks. She accused me of having pre-menstrual syndrome. That son of hers, Ronald, definitely has psychological problems—he called me a basket case. And I'm still recovering from the blow Curtis landed as they were leaving.

"There's a strong possibility I may be bleeding internally," I call as they head towards the waiting taxi.

"Porter Jones," Georgina shrieks from the sidewalk,

"you don't need a true love, you need a fleet of ambulance attendants."

Fortunately, as a Welfare Worker, I am eligible for stress leave at three-quarters of my regular pay. I hate to admit to failing emotions but it's the only way I can get off work to minister to my swollen liver. My doctor has refused to see me. The things I could say about the medical profession.

Before long a person called Wanda follows me home from the health food store.

When I finally speak to her, as a test, I say, "I have this pain."

"People with pain almost always have something wrong in the body," she says and I am ecstatic. I know I have made a match. Wanda clinches it when she says, "I can always tell a victim of 20th Century Disease. You need me."

"Okay," I say. And so to bed.

Wanda is an old hippie: long flowering skirt, hairy legs, several pounds of beads hanging off her neck. She has taken to preparing herbal remedies for me, teas, poultices. She gathers the herbs from her own garden and administers them while chanting and nodding her head towards the eastern sky, her long grey hair falling over her unhinged breasts. And furthermore, she is an excellent masseuse.

"Doctors are rip-off artists," she says.

True. True. True.

We are like-minded, Wanda and I. The things she says about the medical profession. For instance: how come, how come and how come?

How come we can land a man on the moon and we haven't yet found a cure for Agoraphobia?

How come doctors play so much golf while all over the world people are starving for adequate recreational facilities?

How come doctors get all the money while lay people like me are having to shop at the Nearly New and make a cult out of getting by with less?

She also says, "Doctors don't know dick. Anybody can see you're allergic to everything."

To this end Wanda has removed every piece of synthetic material from my house. This activity hasn't left me much. The TV, my dishes, the kitchen table and chairs, my Dacron wall-to-wall, even the plastic toilet roll holder. All sit in a pile on the front lawn. The shower curtain. A windfall for the Sally Ann.

She has painted the interior of my house Maalox-white, using lead-free paint. White walls, white ceilings, white floors. My house looks like the inside of a laboratory. I sleep on a white cotton futon; Wanda allows white cotton pyjamas. She vacuums dust from her naked self before visiting me from the custodial tent outside; she monitors my condition twenty-four house a day.

She brings me cauliflower soup, the cauliflower hand-grown in the finest organic soil.

"Mineral deposits found in cauliflower are effective in treating advanced cancer of the colon," she assures me. Every day the cauliflower cure.

I spend my days wandering through the bare room in an orgy of illness. I've never felt better in my life.

Before long, Wanda sets up a roadside stand and is charging admission.

"Opportunity knocks," she says. "The doctors aren't the only ones to make hay out of gas."

She has called me the Bubble-Man. Sightseers now file through the flower beds and peer in at me through my curtainless living room window. I bask in the attention, their awe-filled eyes caressing me like benevolent heat lamps. Judging from the crowds, Wanda is making a killing.

Lately she tells me that Bubble-Man T-shirts are selling like crazy. She says she is about to become President of Bubble-Man Industries, manufacturers of disease memorabilia: stool samples, vials of blood, plastic throat swabs.

"Okay," I say, "but can you tell me why I am dying? I have this pain."

"In the neck?" Wanda asks.

"All over."

"Well, keep it," she says, "that pain has corporate significance."

"All right," I say, "but get me some ginger ale and some Vick's cough drops, cherry-flavoured. And fix my pillow and rub my back and bring me some magazines and bring me the thermometer. I need all the care I can get and don't you forget it."

"Not on your life," Wanda says.

All the sightseers are wearing white cotton pyjamas. Television networks are plaguing us for prime-time interviews: Bubble-Man has suddenly become an important news item and we are getting offers to do commercial endorsements.

Now everyone I know is gawking at me through the living room window. In envy. Covetousness. Isobel and all her relations. Cousins I never knew I had. Former co-workers. The entire staff from the Department of Welfare. Georgina, Ronald, Curtis, their neighbours from the housing project. No one is immune. All gaze in wonder, mouthing at me through the living room window: "We never know you'd be famous, Porter Jones. We never knew you'd be a person of importance."

Fulfillment on their faces. Tears in their eyes.

My head is spinning. I allow members of fundamentalist religious organisations to touch the hem of my pyjamas.

Cripples and maniacs sit reverentially outside my window. For hours.

But then suddenly the doctors descend. Swarms of them are poring over my body, taking tests, peering in my orifices. "Wanda, Wanda, this wasn't in the plan. You said doctors are the plague of the earth!"

But Wanda's nonplussed. "Things change," she says. "And studies show that businesses which use consultants wisely are more likely to flourish than those which do not. You have to be sensitive to market forces if you want to survive."

So I am charitable to the doctors, serene in my national sickness, swollen with illness-identity. I'll be a good business investment for Wanda. "A barium enema? No problem. Suck on this little metal tube? Delighted."

But when the doctors finish testing me they ponder: how come, how come and how come?

How come Porter Jones has all this attention?

How come he is lying bloated with gas on a cotton futon and is not in one of our technologically advanced medical centres?

How come a businesswoman-hippie has control of this amazing new gimmick when there are research foundations to vie for, new medical centres to be had?

The doctors buy out Wanda's interest in Bubble-Man

Industries and move me to a specially sterilized Bubble-Room at their Centre.

Wanda is pleased with the settlement. "Buy low, sell high," he says as she's leaving. "Besides, I'm onto something. There's this guy, paralyzed from the waist down from eating Aspartame. He needs me."

My bubble has burst. After six weeks of further testing at the Centre, the doctors can find nothing wrong. As well, interest in me is waning; the polls show that VCRs are turning family television viewing into video campfire gatherings. This means that I am no longer being watched—I have achieved viewer saturation. My ability to command the public's attention is no longer significant.

My removal from the medical centre happened this way. I was spending my brief but halcyon days there, as usual, nursing one of my invisible, lurking tumours or else giving interviews through the Plexiglas of my Bubble-Room when a workman burst through the door and began stripping the Saran Wrap from the walls.

"What are you doing?" I gasped. "Don't you know I'm the Bubble-Man? I have 20th Century Disease. I'm allergic to *everything!*"

"Got orders to re-do this room, Mac," was all he would tell me.

Within hours the Bubble-Room had been transformed

to resemble the inside of a church: altar, font, cross, stained glass windows. Six hospital beds done over to look like pews. Three nuns, three priests, all dressed in deathly black, prepared to take up residence.

"Electromagnetic clatter from millions of man-made sources is drowning out the whispers from heaven," they explained. "We're donating ourselves to medical science. Research. Soul transplants. That sort of thing. Please make way for the cameras."

In desperation I called up Georgina. "I'm being turfed out," I wailed, "thrown back to the polluting forces, my only possessions, the white pyjamas on my back, my portable heart monitor. How come, how come and how come?"

Today I have Diverticulitis. Yesterday it was Scabies. Last week, gritty deposits on my tibia. It's incredible the way I go on living.

I have moved in with Georgina; Isobel got the house in our divorce settlement. Because of my many illnesses I am totally unable to work. Fortunately my union at the Welfare Office provides me with a lifelong disability pension at fifty percent of my regular wage. With the money Georgina makes as a Welfare recipient, we get by pretty well, especially since we sent her kids to a group home—all those preadolescent hormones were giving me migraines.

It took a while to adjust to life post-Bubble but I am now, once again, at home with plague, virus and allergic reaction. Still, I am always on the lookout for a new disease which will explain my condition. Unfortunately there is not a doctor in the country who will see me.

Lately I have been troubled with Narcolepsy. I am liable to keel over in mid-sentence. It's like dropping dead, only I fall asleep instead. Nevertheless, I was able to get Georgina pregnant. I can't remember when I did this but she assures me that I am the father and not that ambulance attendant, Arnold, who is always hanging around. "For one last autograph," he winks as I plunge to the ground.

But I have fond thoughts for the child. Maybe if I can hold out through the deterioration of my sight, hearing and appetite which I know is in store for me, and the incontinence and the mental disturbance, as well. Maybe if I am still alive when the child is old enough to realize that studies show/experts say that he was born to die, that living is just a series of unexplained, uncomfortable medical conditions, occurring one after the other, sometimes all at once, perhaps then I will show him my scrapbook. Pages and pages of newspaper clippings from my Bubble-Man days, boxes full of disease souvenirs: the T-shirts and white pyjamas. It may be a distinct advantage for him to go through life with a once-famous father. On the other hand, perhaps I shouldn't influence him unduly—he'll have his own diseases to discover.

TRASHERS

The trashers are hiding in the trees again. Young ones, high up in the English ivy that wraps itself around the oak trees in our yard. I caught sight of one this morning, before everyone was awake, a dark-haired young man slipping from tree to tree. Young Trashers are bolder at first light, rustling through the trees. You'd think it was the stirring of leaves; they're clever at imitating that sound.

But it's the old Trashers you have to watch out for, the male ones who wander about so shamelessly, their huge penises flapping, just barely disguised by their short terry cloth robes. That's in the daytime. At night they hide in closets. Sometimes I've found two, even three of them huddled together behind the dresses in the girls' rooms, an alarming bouquet. A bedtime story, they pretend. A story about long ago, they lie. Oh they're sneaky, the old Trashers. Long ago indeed. They want to prance about naked in front of the children, show off what they can no longer use. Shoo, shoo, we have to shout, and take a broom to them.

The old ones always appear at bedtime, and often old women are hiding in the closets with them. Grandma Trashers. They're wicked. Last winter we found a nest beneath Lisa's bed, five small Grandmas in pastel track suits, chattering away, eating raisin toast. If you don't destroy the nest in time they multiply like gerbils. Pretty soon there's Grandma Trashers everywhere, commandeering the kitchen, feeding the children white sugar, poisoning their minds with tales about spankings, God, and cleaner houses. Oh, they're desperate worms, the Grandma Trashers. The wolf was right to eat them.

You can't be too careful. Because there's the funnymen, too—the Clowns. They're the worst of all, vicious, attacking. The Clowns live on the roof. Each spring they return like starlings (where they spend the winters is anybody's guess). Suddenly they appear with ladders, ten, twelve of them in striped suits and duck feet, and those hideous leering faces. They love to roll down the slope of our roof into vats of runny custard. Laughing, shrieking, they keep it up all day long, a terrible din. The entire spring and summer is lost; we have to keep the curtains drawn or else there's those awful red noses and wide white lips pressed against the window pane grinning at us.

During Clown season Father and I take turns guarding the children's room. At night we have to make sure the windows are locked otherwise the Clowns will sneak in and lure the children away. Once, before we began our nightly vigil, we suffered an assault from Mr. Jam and Bobo the Dwarf. Oh, the turmoil they caused! In the morning we found them in the living room with the children—juggling, somersaulting, pulling coins from their elephant ears. Our tiny girls cartwheeling in a frenzy, knocking the memorial plates off the wall. Our son holding hands with Mr. Jam and spinning, spinning. Their laughter was frightening. The chesterfield knocked on its side, the dining room table lying with its legs up like an awkward dying thing. It took days for Father and me to calm the children; everyone got sick, we nearly lost them.

We're worn out. But that's a parent's job—guarding the children—keeping them covered with the thick blanket of our influence. Father wonders: How much longer? But it may never end because, besides Trashers and Clowns, there's Bad Thoughts. Bad Thoughts are everywhere like swarms of circling gnats attacking our children's minds and if we don't protect them they cry out helplessly: Emancipation! Freedom! Self-Indulgence! You have to be vigilant about everything, even TV nature shows. One horrible episode of *Wild Kingdom* comes to mind, that scene on the beach, whales slaughtering seals. The turmoil that ensued, the upset. We had the children write protest letters to Channel 9: we are sensitive children, they said, we are gentle souls. We wept, they said, such violence, what is this world you are giving us?

An evil world, we tell them, a beguiling place. One that has your family besieged inside this darkened house with Trashers lurking everywhere. With Clowns frolicking on the roof, and now, this very day, ramming umbrellas against the outside walls, hurling custard pies at the windows. Squirting onlookers with false-smelling flowers. Marching on the front lawn waving placards: FREE THE CHILDREN! WHAT ABOUT SCHOOL? Even our fireman's hose is useless against the onslaught, this relentless wave of Trashers and Clowns storming the house, chanting: Children. Children.

Father wonders: How much longer can we hold them off?

THE BRIGHT GYMNASIUM OF FUN

How many laughers make up a laugh track? How are laugh tracks engineered?

Is there a laugh track company? With its own building/parking lot/cafeteria? Does the laugh track company have its own stable of laughers and highly trained technicians? Are laugh track companies union shops? With shop stewards and an annual general meeting? With negotiated contracts covering such items as sick leave for laryngitis and with the right to strike for better working conditions?

Do laughers laugh at anything? At nothing? Is the mark of a good laugher one who can laugh for no reason at all, as if a switch were turned on?

Do laughers practice laughing? Sitting or standing in their living rooms/kitchens/bedrooms or on public transportation systems, do they suddenly ring out with laughter, practicing the same laugh over and over until they get it right? Do professional laughers, therefore, have to carry identification on their persons at all times which will reassure startled or frightened passers-by that they are indeed just practicing their trade and not in fact, mad or dangerous or both?

Is there a pay scale for laughers? Are guffawers, hooters, roarers and howlers paid more for their work than are gigglers, twitters, cacklers and snigglers? Do belly laughers and shriekers command the highest fees, enough to make a decent wage? Enough to claim, in real life, the equivalent of the humorous, middle-class counterpart presented in many of the TV sitcoms they perform for?

What is real life? Is it that state of being which exists other than what is presented on television and in movies and videos? Something other than performance and posture?

Are there child laughers in special demand for childhood laugh track events such as cartoons/birthdays/tooth extractions? And what of amateur laughers? Are there how-to-laugh books developed especially for them which can be purchased at airport magazine shops/drug stores and which encourage them to embrace laughing as a hobby? Are there night school courses that amateur laughers can attend in

January/February/March? Tricks of the trade that they can learn from practitioners who are slightly more skilled at laughing than they are? Techniques such as breath control/crescendo/decrescendo as in the training of singers and musicians? Are there laughing forms to master?

And what of those sad/abnormal souls who stubbornly refuse all merriment, all lamp shade and lewd joke activity? What of them? Should there not be places/institutions/homes where they can receive treatment for their affliction? From which they can emerge, restored to rapture, and armed with their tanks of nitrous oxide to declare that it is *not* better to sorrow than to laugh, it is *not* better to die than be born?

Is it true that the aging process kills off dopamine cells in the brain, why as we get older euphoria declines, and our capacity to have fun diminishes? Why there is no fool like an old fool, young fools being a dime a dozen?

Is there a market, therefore, for personal, portable laugh tracks? Small, special recording devices that we can all carry around? Attach to our persons? To enable us to laugh at our families/governments/worlds? Would illness/despair/hopelessness/anguish finally vanish as some people have suggested? Would we then all be prodded into states of chronically good moods, becoming perpetually pleased, and not tormented to death as we are now with the what-fors and whys of an absurd existence?

Would the boundaries, then, not melt away between

what is laughable and what is not? With everyone wearing their portable laugh tracks and laughing at everything/nothing, even in their dreams, even in love, would not the world as we know it become like one enormous California, all smooth and mild as a grapefruit? A heaven on earth? A bright gymnasium of fun?

On the other hand, in a world of stunned, uniform laughers would there not emerge a deviant subclass, a deliberately unfunny, underground movement of anti-laughers declaring their right to misery/bleakness/doom? Intent on the destruction of stand-up comincs and game show hosts? Would not the cry of dadaist ecstasy be heard again, this time as "Assassinate the Laughers!" in an updated attempt to startle/shock the smiling millions who, poised before their television screens, are laughing on cue as if possessed by some grand/homeric/universal tic?

Should not television laugh tracks be scrutinized? Do they not control the quality/frequency/duration of our laughter? Do they not disallow transcendence by rendering all experience cute? Do they not tranquilize us by keeping us calm, by rendering our laughter thin and meaningless until death do us part?

What if the laugh track laughers went on strike? How would any of us know what is funny?

BED

Who are all these dead people at the foot of my bed? They're shoving one another, three old women and a small skinny boy all trying to push one another off my bed. The boy is crying, shrieking. Why does no one come? Four dead people shouldn't be here, they should be on their own beds. I'd get up and bite them but I haven't got the strength. Why won't they leave me alone? They're laughing at me, crawling up the bed, trying to get my purse. I'm scared if I shout they'll grab me, push me into the sea. The sky overhead is blue. I'm sitting in a deck chair beside my mother; she's wearing pearls, a summer dress. Smile, she's saying, you needn't look so glum, life's a song, there's still time left to sing it. Overhead a spotlight, maybe that's the sun. I'm old, my eyesight blurs. No, it's a light, switching on, switching off. Don't tell me the dead don't speak. My mother stands at the foot of the bed. Hold my hand, she's saying, the journey ahead is smooth and long. There are four dead people in a rowboat bobbing in the sea. Hurry up, jump in, they're calling. Why does no one come? I wish the dead were people I knew. Instead the light keeps switching on, switching off. My mother's swimming towards the foot of my bed. Come on, come on. I can't swim past these pillows, I'm crying, I haven't got the strength. My mother's in the water waving, splashing. The water feels so warm. Come on you silly girl, jump in. The dead are cheering wildly, mouths of rust at me, mouths of dust. It's time. It's time. It's time.

SONG FOR LEONARD COHEN

I. THE TOOTH OF THE LION

Leonard Cohen was leaning against a white wall with his girlfriend. Upon seeing me he turned to her and said, "Ah, here comes a tough little man with a three on his back."

I said, "It is only that I am packaged small," and I bowed.

"The three," Leonard said to his girlfriend, "means that he can take orders from above or else lying on his back. You see one and two makes three."

"Wrong," I said. "I am three because I chase wild animals and it's the lion that I'm after. God leaves lion chasers alone."

Just then a lion ran orange through the sparkling blue sea.

"My," said Leonard Cohen, "your lion looks like a Sear's oil painting," and he laughed and stroked his girlfriend's hair and made a poem that shrieked at mundane things.

But then he remembered that other poem, 'Love is like the lion's tooth,' and a poem about fierce dancing took seed in his heart.

2. THE REPEATING ROUTINE

Leonard Cohen was leaning against a white wall with his girlfriend. He held a pencil in his mouth like a rose.

Gertrude Stein walked by and said, "I hear they're going to make a musical out of my life."

"Who's playing you?" asked Leonard Cohen, and gave the pencil to his girlfriend who fainted.

"Mitzi Gaynor," said Gertrude Stein, "but she can't get the repeating right."

Leonard Cohen explained to the unconscious form at his feet. "It's the tap routines. That blanket skirt that Mitzi has to wear makes it difficult for dancing."

"Wrong," said Gertrude Stein. "There is always in everyone repeating, there is always in everyone beginning and ending, there is always in everyone stupid being, there is always then sometimes some one to everyone and Mitzi Gaynor is not to me."

Just then a chorus line of middle-aged women in grey business suits can-canned by.

"You see," Gertrude Stein said of the women, "there is only middle-repeating," and she shook her head sadly and began to walk away.

"Wait," Leonard called, for he was on the trail of a poem about Christ. "Look at it this way. There is living and dying, beginning and ending. I'm just in my middle-living while your life ended long ago, yet your words still go on repeating and some can remember something of such a life."

"Sounds familiar," said Gertrude Stein suspiciously, and then she laughed and slapped Leonard Cohen on the back. "Good for you," she said, and swam towards the empty distance.

3. THE DANCE IS ENDING

Leonard Cohen was leaning against a white wall with his girlfriend. He was dreaming a dream about ending.

Upon seeing me he said, "I want your youngest child," and he bowed.

"But she's only three years old," I answered, and looked for a chorus line to hide in.

"I want your youngest child," he repeated, "and I will give you my house in return. It is a long low house with a view," he said, and stroked his girlfriend's hand. She dissolved like steam over water.

I decided to look at his house. It was on top of a hill and it hugged the rock like a barnacle.

"But the view is facing the wrong way," I complained. "Your house only looks at the backs of things."

Just then a monster ran through the door and spat my daughter from its mouth. She crawled to Leonard's wall. He touched her new blonde hair.

"You see, she's nearly mine," he said, and I imagined the horrible stuff of dreams. I imagined him feeding on her soul.

Then Leonard's eyes turned white and his face took on a sudden sadness. He wept 'til his tears made music.

So I took my child. I bundled her beneath my coat and carried her off like a secret. I ran through his darkness like a blindman but my daughter struggled hard against me. At last she broke free.

"Let me go," she screamed, and reached back towards him with the strong, yearning arms of a lover, ravishing for the kill.

4. THE ROAR OF THE LION

Leonard Cohen was leaning against a white wall with his girlfriend. There were lions in the trees.

He felt cold breath and looked to my child who was dancing.

"Keep the dancing gay," he said. "Keep it mad ravishing Mary gay dancing 'round her lover before the ghastly kill."

Just then a crack, large as a heart beat, tore through his wall.

"Only the wind through a window," Leonard laughed, and reached for his girlfriend who had vanished. "Just the window, not the broken brain giving air this time," he said, and covered himself with a poem.

But this time the cold air hung over him and swirled around his feet like Autumn. It cooled his forearms, his neck. It smelled his nose shivering in his hot poet body and blew all dancers from his breast. It grabbed his soul and flung in from his hot, impassioned mouth. It filled his mind with torment.

It was the lion roaring.

SHED

I've built this shed. A pleasant enough building, don't you think? A plain, square structure, twelve by fourteen feet on a cement slab. Covered with cedar siding and a duroid roof. I insisted on the slab having no idea how long I'll be here, otherwise the winter damp will seep in. I've even made a curtain for the one window from some material left over from when we had the house. Remember the house?

I like the bed you sent over, by the way, the cot. It suits my vigil very well. And the dog, I do appreciate the dog. Dumb company is about all I'm up to.

I know you consider it a rash act, the act of a mad

woman, but I've been visiting the edge of this great hole for so long I decided to move here permanently. And about before—you must agree I did my best. My effort was not without merit, paving all about me with reasons, busyness.

Now I'm comfortable. My shed has everything I need: a hot plate, electric heat and, of course, the weekly groceries which you so generously provide. There are not many husbands who would do as much.

It's true the hole is larger than I expected. But my shed is in no danger of slipping in even though it's situated at the hole's edge. A smooth, seamless edge, like the edge of a waterfall, quite unsuspecting. Think of all those trusting souls who might tumble in unawares if I were not here to keep watch. Children, even, swallowed up before their time.

Remember our lives together? How even though the years were bright we still found time to fear the worst? The victimization of our children, the failing livers of those we loved, the awful secrets we had about each other whispered to friends over telephones, the awful knowledge we carried, the subtext surfacing. Finding ways to remind us that life is bizarre, that this is our natural condition. How we confined that knowledge, so rigorous we were in its suppression, until all that remained was a small black pit within our stomachs, a continual achiness.

Now I wear that knowledge like an old black coat.

Since my residency here I have discovered that the hole

expands and contracts slightly, like a tide, although it doesn't appear to be affected by the moon's journey. I am tempted to say that it breathes but that wouldn't be accurate either. This great black weight existing on either side of us like bookends. It gets larger as one gets older. Did you know that?

STREET

You ought to write a story, my story, about the desperation I feel about things ending. About the way we make a big deal about crossing the street, holding hands laughing, watching out for wild cars. About how some of us don't make it. The way chance always gets the other guy. How I got to my camper that time before the storm hit, the only one for miles around who made it. So what? Before disaster struck. So what? Take a picture of me running across the street. I'm the one who made it. What for? I'm the one who didn't get wasted too soon. Tell my story. About how my face is good looking even with my hair wet. About my three kids always on my back. One time I told them: leave me alone for a month, don't even knock on my door. They're grown up, should be taking care of themselves by now. But they all ended up back in my bed. Here I am worrying myself sick about things ending and they can't even begin. And my old aunt, my mother, my sister. Tell about them all joining hands, still making a big fuss about crossing the street laughing with the thrill of it. We've all got short legs, big behinds. So what? Then there's my husband. Every day I get out of the shower he's waiting, hanging around the shower curtain, licking his lips, clenching his fingers. You'd think I was some babe. I'm fifty-one, got veins the size of ropes hanging off my legs. Tell my story. About the way he's always grabbing my box, twisting my nipples every time I get out of the shower. You'd think my body was some weird spaceship he's riding, flying out the window of our three-bedroom bungalow. Gone. Can't wait to get started. Can't wait can't wait can't never wait. Tell how first I'm a container for the kids then next a spaceship for the husband. My story. About the panic I feel about things ending. About the cruel, sad joke. How you always get it through the heart. My hope, how it's scattered like ashes. How I close my eyes now when I cross the street. Tell about that. How when the time comes I won't even know which wild car hit me.

THE DONALD BARTHELME TOURING CAR WASH

The Donald Barthelme Touring Car Wash stopped at the Elbow, Saskatchewan Food-A-Rama and took us by surprise. There was just the one car, an old blue Chev, and inside were Donald and his five sons. We'd heard they were roaming the country, stopping at shopping center parking lots to wash cars if they could, but sightings had been rare. The last thing we expected was his arrival in our own small town.

I was out shopping that morning with my small son Errol and it was a lucky thing; we might have missed them. We watched the car pull into the parking lot and the five boys jump out, run around to the trunk and pull out buckets, rags and a bottle of liquid soap. One boy ran off with a hose in search of water.

Then the driver got out, an older guy in glasses, disheveled-looking, wearing soiled gray sweats and wine-coloured vinyl slippers. That's how I knew for sure it was Donald Barthelme—those trademark slippers. They say he wears them everywhere now so he'll always feel at home in the world.

They also say that Donald Barthelme is a bug case but I don't believe them. Just because he tacks story ideas to his back with scotch tape so that his back is always covered. . . . Just because he flutters when he walks, sounding like those plastic flags at car lots that snap in the wind . . .

When I saw him he only rustled, but maybe that's because the prairie wind that day was sleeping. Watching Donald Barthelme walk into the store, Errol said, "He looks like a furry white tree."

His sons lost no time washing cars; soon the parking lot was awash in soap suds. I think they might have made a few bucks.

Donald Barthelme didn't look pleased or anything when he came out of the store carrying a plastic bag full of oranges. The line of clean cars didn't mean a thing to him, he didn't even give them a glance. Just got in his car and started up the engine. That got his sons running, stashing their hoses in the trunk, and their pails and their wash cloths, and then they all took off in a hurry, heading west, moving on towards Regina. Whew. It was all over before we knew it. Errol and I just stood dumbstruck by the side of our pick-up. Donald Barthelme had whizzed by like an idea you can't quite get hold of.

But a piece of paper had fallen from his back as he was getting into the car. It lay in a puddle of soap suds and I raced over to see what it might tell me. Something about leaving our messages chewed onto the sides of pencils but that's all I could make out, the rest being unintelligible, soaked through as it was.

They say Donald Barthelme is dead but I don't believe that either. There have been enough sightings of him by now to prove the opposite and not just in grocery store parking lots either. Truckers have reported seeing his car, stopped by the side of the road. They've seen a man surrounded by a group of boys tacking pieces of paper onto his back. There's even a song about it playing on the country and western stations in the midwest. Donald Barthelme's been seen by widows, too, in discount stores buying pencils, five for a dollar. One time he appeared at a Legionnaires' convention and read some erotic poems. Death came swiftly to several in the audience.

As for me, that morning in the Food-A-Rama parking lot was the only time I ever saw him. But I'm always on the look out. Meanwhile I tag along on my own life, wearing my new wine-coloured vinyl slippers, hanging over my backyard fence, chewing on pencils. Hoping for glimpses of Donald Barthelme in the tiniest of situations: soap suds, freeway traffic, the Swedish army, anything.

THE EARLY PLASTIC SHRINE

Everything went wrong for the Christmas Party. I got a spot on my liver and had to go to the hospital for tests. By the time they were through with me I was an hour and a half late. Trying to dress was impossible—I couldn't remember how to do it, what went with what. My blue stockings had a tear up the left leg; I put a red top with an orange bottom. Then as I mounted the stairs to my party I had an orgasm on each step. This slowed things up considerably.

Finally I arrived, two hours late for my own party. The jazz trio from the Indian Reserve was not doing well, no one could hear them, they were performing away from the crowd, towards the air and the trees. Someone in the crowd yelled out, "They stink!" then half the guests left. Meanwhile I realized that most of the guests were relatives of in-laws I did not like. Who invited them? I wondered. None of my friends were there. Who invited these semi-strangers and all these eleven-year-old boys eating up the cakes?

My husband said, "We're out of avocados," which meant there could be no more Tex-Mex and I hadn't even started the chili which was to be served in half an hour's time.

I decided to leave. On my way out I heard a conversation between a neighbour and my mother-in-law standing beside her yellow convertible. "I wouldn't bother with the party," my mother-in-law was saying, "chances are the toilet bowl hasn't even been cleaned."

So I visited my friend the priest. He'd just come off a long shift with a dead man. "I thought that soul would never leave," he said, "it just kept flying around the kitchen like a piece of white blubber, banging into the cupboards, scaring the budgie."

We made love on his colonial chesterfield. Outside, snow was falling, one perfect flake at a time.

The priest said to me, "Christmas is a good time to die. I can always tell when a soul is ready to leave a dead man, it begins with the eyes. The furrows between the brows become a canyon and the eyes pale and stare almost erotically."

While he kissed me, warts grew on my lips.

I spent the rest of the night at the Early Plastic Shrine of Leo H. Baekland in Yonkers, New York. There, beneath a giant replica of a bobbin end made in 1912 by combining clean phenolic resin with formaldehyde to create the first truly synthetic plastic, I slept.

I dreamed I was a child of the mid-twentieth century, waiting around for science fiction to come true. I was riding in my personal helicopter—the traffic in the heavens was so congested that fleeing souls were crashing into helicopter blades like demented seagulls.

The pillage was awful: priests by the submarine load had to be called in to place wreaths of plastic bananas at the grave sites.

Leo H. Baekland invited me to dinner. We sat down on the roof of his two-story laboratory to carve a turkey dinner the size of a gelatine capsule.

"There is nothing new under the sun," he said, handing me my half of the pill.

"Not true," I wailed. "Don't I have *Science Digest?* Isn't something new promised every month? And right here beside the ad for fibre optics, doesn't it promise new worlds, new suns?"

"New things are treacherous," said Leo H. Baekland, "newly invented things insisting on the future. Possibly we could have done without plastic."

Suddenly I was having a nightmare. It was frightening

to think of living on without some wonderful anticipation, some happy surprise, some new gadget.

I stood at the end of a long black tunnel and shouted to my friend, the priest, and to Leo H. Baekland: "Waiting around for science fiction to come true is a lot more satisfying than waiting around for death." I was crying.

Their laughter cut the night like a musical saw. "Booze, God, technological fixes, it's all the same to us," they said.

The doctor woke me up.

"Here," he said, removing me from the Early Plastic Shrine, "we'll just attach this plastic tubing to your brain and pump you full of someone new to be. It won't take long and I believe you're an isolated case. I don't believe that what you've got is easily transmitted. You'll be back at your party in no time."